BEST HOTWIFE EROTICA VOL. I

Friends and Lovers

LACEY CROSS   PAUL GARLAND   SEAN GEIST

KIRSTEN MCCURRAN   MAX SEBASTIAN

DELORES SWALLOWS   KENNY WRIGHT

Edited by

KIRSTEN MCCURRAN

APHRODITE
OMNIMEDIA

CONTENTS

YES WOMAN

Max Sebastian

The real trouble didn't start until July 4.

It was our turn to host this year's gathering. I'd been hoping for a manageable event, but this year we had a whole load of family and friends – including a surprising turnout from my old college buddies.

"You were right," Mark said as I showed him through to our backyard, where people were gathering around our new swimming pool. "It was a long way to come — but we can spend a few days up here, you know? Head into the City, see the sights."

Mark brought his whole family with him — wife and three kids. Barney had the new baby. Jim and Minnie flew in all the way from California. A smattering of my wife's old friends from school came, too. But given our circumstances, it wasn't any of them that worried me.

Robbie worried me. Here he was, freshly divorced, his tan still blazing from the singles cruise he'd just been on.

"Man, it was *fantastic*. You should've seen how much tail there was on that damn boat."

"Katie would never want to go on a cruise," I said. "She can't handle it if she's anywhere she can't see land."

Robbie patted me on the shoulder. "If she came with me, she'd never get her head up long enough to see there's no land," he said with a wicked grin. I humored him with a tepid smile.

I'd never worried about Robbie before – even with his turbulent relationship history. But this time, I had cause to feel nervous that he was here.

Life had changed for Katie and me recently. In some ways for the better, sure.

Barney was the first to notice the new SUV in the driveway. "When did you get a new car?"

"Last week. It was on order for six months."

"You guys must be doing pretty well for yourselves — I mean, you got the XRE model there and everything."

I sighed. "Not as well as we'd like. Not with those trade tariffs still in place."

The ball dropped when I showed him the backyard.

"A new *pool* as well? What the—?"

"And a new roof," I said. "And a landscaping firm to make everything look nice."

"It looks amazing, man. So why the big splurge?"

Another sigh. "Katie joined a cult."

"She joined a *what now*?" Barney spit out his beer at that one.

"Well, it might as well be a cult. A few months ago, this motivational speaker was at the Country Club. She wasn't even going to go, but then one of her friends was organizing it, so..."

Barney nodded. "And this *motivated* her to buy loads of stuff?"

"The guy was all about people saying 'yes' to everything. Like in that Jim Carrey movie a while back? I mean, *Jesus*. But for some reason, it really stuck with Katie. She decided things around here had gotten a little stale..."

"I guess you have to be pretty motivational if you're gonna make a living as a motivational speaker."

I laughed. "Yeah. But Katie has pledged to say 'yes' to any direct question for a whole year."

"Jesus, *no*."

"Jesus, yes."

Naturally, the subject of Katie's pledge got around the party relatively quickly. However, there was a clear difference in the way the different groups of our friends and family treated the subject.

Family members, for the most part, were all very impressed with Katie's new drive and productivity—that she was doing various projects for the PTA now, she was learning how to play tennis at the Country Club, she'd been promoted at work because she'd been taking on so much stuff.

"And both your kids seem so happy all the time…"

"Well, of course they are. She keeps taking them to McDonald's all the time. And the movie theater. And last weekend, we went to Florida, for God's sake. Disney."

"Well, I think it's *lovely*."

I tried not to be a Debbie Downer about it. Nobody wanted to hear the bad stuff. The fact that Katie had very little spare time these days. That she made the rest of us feel lazy. The notion that she had been somewhat miserable with her life until she started doing all this stuff. The fact that the kids were eating crap because they'd discovered that mom would take them to McDonald's if they simply asked her to.

This whole 'yes' thing was really not suitable for a young family.

Katie's friends were all strangely eager to learn from her about everything to do with the 'Just Say Yes' program. All of them imagining how their lives might go if they did the same.

"So, you just say 'yes' to everything?"

"Yeah, pretty much."

"What if you don't have time to do it?"

"You say you'll do it the next time you're available… if you truly can't possibly do it for somebody, then they might say it's okay, I'll get someone else…"

"But if you do have time available to do it, but you *really* don't want to?"

"Well, then you have to do it."

I guess we were all hitting middle age, that time of our lives that was ripe for a mid-life crisis. Katie's friends were interested in anything that might shake things up. I couldn't say I wholly disapproved of Katie's new life philosophy. It was nice to have a new car. A swimming pool. The trip to Disney had been fun. There was definitely a plus side to the whole Live For The Present mentality.

My friends weren't interested in learning from anybody. And they weren't even considering taking up that kind of pledge themselves. But they were undoubtedly fascinated by the whole thing, just as much as anybody at the party that day.

"She's buying anything people ask her to? I mean, shit, that must be a hell of a lot."

"I have to check her email two or three times a day," I nodded. "And I have ultra-premium platinum levels of spam blocking on her computer. But, you know… she gets a phone call from the Police Benevolent Fund… or some guy saying he could build us a new swimming pool within six weeks…"

"It's a great pool, man."

"Thanks."

Robbie, naturally, was interested in what her limits might be. "So… if I asked her to go buy a rifle and shoot somebody… she'd do it?"

I said, "I think she draws the line when it comes to breaking the law."

"No law against shooting somebody in the leg."

"Uh… *yeah*. There is. Definitely a law against that one."

"If I asked her to do my taxes, would she?"

"Probably, yes. But you might end up with a visit from the IRS…"

Well, so far, so manageable. After a few hours, I was pleasantly surprised that things did settle down, and conversations moved on to other things. There was food, and drinks, and an inflatable castle for the youngest guests, and people were having fun.

Later, there were even fireworks. We could all sit back and relax and watch the show the Country Club put on in the golf course behind our yard.

The real fireworks of the night, though, were yet to come.

———

People began to head home once the pyrotechnics were done.

Those with younger kids were gone by nine o'clock.

Our kids went to stay with Grandma and Grandpa, which was hugely helpful. It meant Katie and I could relax a little while the key struggles of hosting were winding down.

The party evolved to the point that my friends and I were down in the basement — the *Man Cave* — watching Super Bowl re-runs and drinking beers around the pool table. Katie and her friends were out by the pool, sipping wine and enjoying the stars over the golf course.

It was actually Katie's friends who first started talking about how her Just Say Yes Pledge could affect our marriage.

At about elevenish, I had to go upstairs to get more beer to restock the fridge in the basement. I went through the kitchen, out the side door, and then into the garage to pick up another crate of Bud.

"No, not at work."

"*Seriously?*"

Hmm… So, it turned out that I could hear the conversation on the patio from the back of the garage.

My wife was saying, "If I told everybody at work, they'd keep asking me to do loads more work. I'd probably never get home at night."

I gave an eyeroll at that, considering the number of late evenings Katie had at work already since she began her Just Say Yes program.

"And you'd probably get half the scuzz-buckets in the company hitting on you, asking you out for a drink," Katie's friend Mary-Lou said.

"Yeah, there is that," Katie laughed.

"But what if one of them *did*?"

I didn't recognize that voice. Sylvia, maybe? Penny?

"One of them did what?"

"Someone comes up and asks you out for a drink after work?"

Katie said, "Then I'd probably have to say 'yes' and go out for a drink with him."

Wow.

I stopped in my tracks hearing that. Funnily enough, I'd never even thought about the possibility that some guy could hit on my wife, and under her current policy, she might have to accept whatever he asked her to do.

She'd only talked about going out for a drink with a guy, but suddenly I was standing there in the garage with a racing heartbeat and a fully erect cock. What was *that* about?

Katie said, "Everybody at work knows I'm married. And, you know, I have my *wedding ring* on."

"Everyone in *my* office knows *I'm* married," said the person I was thinking was actually Simone. "But *I* still get guys asking me out."

Mary-Lou said, "What if some guy asks you out for a drink... and then while you're out, he keeps asking if you want another drink?"

"Well, then the evening would go on longer than I'd prefer."

"And if he says, would you like to go back to his place…?"

There was a pause. Katie said, "I think by then I would have revealed that I'm doing this program. That I'm only out with him because I couldn't say 'no.' And that I'm very happy with my husband, thank you very much…"

At this point, the relief was palpable. For the first time since I'd started listening in on this conversation, I was able to breathe. I was thankful Katie thought enough of our marriage to say that.

But then Simone said, "You think that would stop a guy from asking to sleep with you?"

God. Now my heart was skipping and my hard-on was throbbing inside my pants.

Why was I so strangely excited about the prospect of my wife being with another man — and being asked to do something wicked?

There was another pause. Then Katie said, "I would hope there wouldn't be anybody at our company that would want me to do something to break my wedding vows."

I breathed again. And yet, somehow, I felt disappointed. Why would I feel disappointment thinking about my wife turning down a guy like that?

I was baffled at my own response to the thought of Katie being unfaithful. Why was I so turned on by the idea of some guy at her company asking her out for a drink? Why did I want to pull out my cock and beat off when I thought about the possibility that she would go back to some guy's place with him because he asked her to?

I snapped out of my daze when I heard one of Katie's friends saying, "If your husband asked you if you were having an affair, you'd have to say 'yes,' so…"

Katie said, "I wouldn't have to say 'yes' if it wasn't true…"

And Simone said, "But if it *was* true?"

At that moment, I heard one of my friends out in the kitchen calling for me. I had to go. I took the beer with me and found Mark out there — my friends had wondered why I was taking so long to get more booze.

———

It was past one am by the time my wife's friends left, and Katie came down to the basement to see why the heck my friends were still there.

Free beer — that was the obvious answer.

But when my wife came downstairs, it reminded my friends of the whole Katie-Only-Saying-Yes thing all over again. None of them had had a chance to talk to her about it directly. They'd only talked to me about it so far.

"So, if we asked you to go rob the bank on Main Street…"

"I already told you: I don't have to do something if it's illegal."

"If I asked you to drive to California and buy a condo with an ocean view…?"

"I would say sure, when I'm next able to do so…"

My friends were desperate to find some loophole that would force Katie to violate her pledge. She seemed to find it amusing, so she wasn't attempting to escape. She just made herself comfortable on one of the couches around the TV and flashed me the occasional sideways glance that said, *your friends are crazy*.

I resisted the temptation to point out that her friends had been grilling her on the chances of her cheating on me with a guy from work. I wasn't supposed to know about that.

Strangely, though there was a risk that my friends would find a way to get my wife to do something she wouldn't usually want to do, I liked having her down there with them. For some strange reason, the conversation she'd had with her friends had made me notice how attractive she was. Perhaps

I'd been taking her for granted far too much in recent years, but now I'd had my eyes opened.

And my eyes were also opened to how my friends were attracted to Katie. I hadn't really noticed it before, but now that she was down here with us, they were kind of flirting with her. Was this because of her program?

She seemed to like it, too.

I felt oddly aroused. I wanted them to flirt with her. I also wanted to take her upstairs and have my wicked way with her — in a way I hadn't for years. And don't get me wrong, there was nothing wrong with our sex life. But I hadn't felt that kind of desire for my wife for a long while.

Anyway.

My friends soon figured out that Katie wouldn't do anything that was categorically impossible — "If I asked you to spend the rest of your life working on developing a time machine, would you?"

She wouldn't vote for somebody because one of my friends asked her to. "I think you can get prosecuted for trying to force somebody to vote for somebody," she said.

"We wouldn't be forcing you…"

"I think I could prove to a judge that you were forcing me to either violate my pledge or vote for somebody I didn't want to…"

She would happily do fairly trivial things like passing them another beer or going up to the kitchen to get more snacks. But after a few of those requests, my friends were bored of that game. They couldn't seem to think of any requests that were significant, and yet doable.

And then Robbie — of course it was Robbie — said, "Katie. If I asked you to kiss me, would you?"

———

I caught my breath.

Katie raised her eyebrows in alarm and looked over at me.

I shrugged. What was I supposed to say?

"I'd hope you wouldn't, Robbie," Katie told him. "I mean… you know I'm married to your *friend*…"

"I know," Robbie said, wandering over from the pool table to the couches. "But you know… if you let the world know about your new philosophy… guys will try it on."

I could see something flickering in Katie's eyes. A kind of realization. A glance at me — *can you believe this guy?* But I was thinking, *how come I hadn't thought of this?* All it would take would be for one guy at work to hit on her, and she'd be forced to choose between violating her program pledge or doing something to seriously affect our relationship.

Robbie said, "I mean… if I was *really* asking you to kiss me, you wouldn't have to break the law…"

"I'd have to break my wedding vows."

"Did your wedding vows say no kissing other guys?"

"It said I'd be faithful to my husband."

"But it didn't define 'faithful'."

Christ. Katie looked at me again, and I thought how stunningly beautiful she was. I felt this strange change come over me. I don't know how to explain it. Maybe it wasn't a change — perhaps it was a realization. For some reason, I wanted Robbie to ask her. I wanted Katie to feel she had to kiss him if she wanted to keep the faith with her cult.

I wanted the two of them to kiss — and enjoy it.

What was going on? I could feel my manhood thickening in my pants.

Katie glanced at me again. I think she expected me to come to her aid. To stop my friends from asking her for sexual favors.

But I was a little drunk, a little confused by my feelings. I didn't like to tell my wife what she could or could not do. And I did feel that if she was going to learn the lesson of what dangers could lurk out there if she decided to stand by this crazy pledge of hers, she'd be better off learning it with someone we knew well.

There was a moment of silence where it almost seemed like the world around us was on pause.

Then Robbie solemnly asked, "Okay. Katie, will you please kiss me?"

Katie sighed and brushed her hand through her long, honey-blonde hair. She glared at me, seemingly annoyed that I was just sitting there. Angry at me because it had come to this.

Then she took a breath and pulled herself to her feet.

"Sure," she said, flashing a taunting glance my way. Willing me to stop her doing this.

Robbie gave me a look, too, which said *I can't believe this is happening.*

But he took a couple of steps toward Katie, too. Towering over her. She reached up to him and planted a little peck on his lips.

He was disappointed by that.

Katie grinned. "You just asked for a *kiss…*" she said.

Then Robbie said, "Katie, will you give me a real, deep, long, *French kiss,* please?"

My wife paused on her way back to her seat, then turned to look at me. My heart was thumping in my chest.

I said, "Uh… look, Robbie…"

Robbie stood his ground. "I *asked* her…"

Katie gave me an eyeroll. I sighed. What did she want me to do? Turf my friends out of our house because they weren't playing nice? I guess she did, but I hesitated.

I don't know. Maybe I wanted to see if she'd really do it.

Maybe I wanted her to fail this stupid thing and go back to normal.

Katie stood up. I could tell I'd upset her. She had wanted me to step in and order Robbie to take back his request. She wanted me to help her keep her ridiculous pledge in the face of this obvious challenge.

But there was a flicker of something in her eyes — a glint that said she might enjoy this.

Maybe she'd find a way to have a little fun punishing me for not getting angry at my friend's audacity and disrespect.

So, she stepped over to Robbie again. This time, she reached an arm up, curled her hand slowly and seductively around the back of his neck, and drew him down for a long, sensual, and *deep* kiss.

Jesus.

I felt breathless. My cock was stiff as a board and *pulsing* between my thighs.

It was so bizarre – and yet so inexplicably erotic – to watch my friend making out with my beautiful wife right in front of us all.

———

Okay, now I was up on my feet. I felt obligated. My friends were looking at me, like, are you just going to sit there and take this?

I would have sat there and taken this — I wanted to.

But I still had my pride, I guess.

Katie still had her arms around Robbie's neck after granting his request. She stayed there with him, gazing into his eyes, smiling sweetly. Flushed.

I felt a flicker of fear — jealousy? Something.

But I sensed this was Katie drawing out the moment for dramatic value, to emphasize how she could punish me if I didn't protect her new pledge from being spoiled by awful men.

I guess it had its effect. Pretty soon, I was ushering all my friends out of my house. "Come on, then, time to go… We've all had plenty to drink… we've all had a nice time… it's getting late…"

It was pretty late. Things had gotten weird. My friends knew why I was shoving them out of the house. They all went obediently. They were even cheerful — they'd found a loophole to get my wife to do things she wouldn't ordinarily do. They had their victory.

As I watched them go from the front door, I realized Robbie was still down in the basement with Katie. My stomach lurched, and my mind jumped to the conclusion that the two of them could easily be down there violating her wedding vows again.

My body — my cock — felt jubilant that my wife had done this crazy thing, making out with my friend. But my rational side was horrified. And terrified it was happening some more.

To my enormous relief, as I approached the basement steps, there was Robbie. Laughing about something with Katie. She didn't seem angry with him at all. In fact… she was kind of flirty with him as she escorted him up the steps and with me to the front door.

"You need to go home and take a *cold shower*, Mister," she was saying, brushing her long, golden hair like she hoped he'd notice it.

Robbie smiled at her like a faithful Labrador, totally under her spell. Then he flashed an apologetic glance my way. I shrugged, indicating _no big deal_. I appreciated his attempt to break my wife from her idiotic cult.

We even shared a bro hug.

The front door closed, leaving me alone with my beautiful wife.

I hadn't wanted her this badly for months. Maybe years.

I thought she might berate me for letting my friends treat her that way, but when I turned back to her, she looked all apologetic, perhaps even worried that she'd done something to actually risk our marriage.

"I'm so *sorry*, I..." she said, her voice oddly shrill.

She was panicking a little, I realized. She had put her self-help program before her marriage.

I said, "It's okay..." and pulled her toward me. She came willingly. We kissed, just as she and Robbie had done. She was hesitant at first, and it made me realize we didn't often just kiss anymore, not like this. Our relationship had long since settled into a state where, if either of us needed sex, we just had sex — we rarely beat around the bush with foreplay. We didn't need to kiss to tell each other we loved each other, so maybe we didn't do it enough anymore. It was skip-to-the-end most of the time.

But right now, I was hungry for her.

I breathed her in and tasted her lips, and my hands found their way to her beautifully shaped derriere. It took her a startled moment to realize what I was doing — that I did, indeed, *want* her. Badly. And then she got into it herself, sucking on my lips in return, pressing her body against mine.

"*What's... going on...?*" she asked breathlessly between feverish kisses.

"What do you think's going on?"

She furrowed her brow briefly. "Well... it's *nice*...?" she said, apparently not wanting to stop me, though she was confused about where my sudden passion came from.

I'm not saying I wasn't also confused about where it came from. But I wasn't going to question it just now.

"Grandma and Grandpa have the kids, so we're on our own..." I pointed out, one of my hands finding her breasts.

"Mmm..." she moaned, smiling despite her confusion. "But they take the kids plenty of times..."

I had my hand up her top, groping her gorgeous breasts over her bra, my fingers delving underneath the material to find her stiff nipples.

Her hand found the hardness lurking in my pants. I heard her gasp as I kissed her soft neck. "You're so hard…"

For a moment, I could tell two and two were being added up to make four. She just stood there, groping the bulge in my jeans.

"Is this because of what I did with Robbie?" she asked, breathless, gazing at me with those emerald green eyes.

I chuckled. "I don't have to say 'yes' to every question someone asks me…"

But she took that as a yes. Her face brightened, her lips curled up in a delighted yet mischievous smile. "You liked it when I kissed him?"

I kissed her mouth again, and this time there was a sudden desperation in her — to suck my lips, to delve her tongue in my mouth, to get my cock out of my pants and into her hands.

Apparently amazed by all this, she sank to her knees before me. She unfastened my fly and hauled down my jeans. She took my big, hard cock in her hands — and then directed it to her mouth.

Oh my God.

It felt so good. She sank down onto my shaft, her hot mouth engulfing my sensitive glans. I groaned as she sucked on me, as she swirled her tongue around my cock. As she squeezed the base of my shaft in her hand.

When was the last time my wife went down on me? I couldn't even remember.

But now she was moaning as she bobbed down on my manhood, apparently enjoying it as much as I was. Turned on by how turned on I was.

I asked her, "If Robbie had asked you, right then and there, to get down on your knees and suck his cock, would you have done it?"

She moaned and bobbed down on my cock a couple more

times. Then she withdrew and gazed up at me with a smile. "I think, maybe, I would have had to."

I leaned down, stroked her cheek with a hand, and kissed her mouth deeply — as though rewarding her for what she'd said. She moaned and kissed me back as though rewarding me for putting that thought out there about her doing this with Robbie.

"Would you have just let me do it?" she asked me as I finally straightened up again.

"I wouldn't want you to have to violate your pledge..."

She squeezed my cock in her hands. "Would you watch while your wife sucked your friend's cock right in front of you?"

"If you were doing it in front of me, I think I'd have to."

She sucked my cock back into her mouth, and I could tell she was imagining it was Robbie. That she was doing this in front of me. It was so hot.

She said, "What if he said he wanted to sleep with me?"

I fought with my own body to keep from coming inside her mouth. It was the hottest sex we'd had in years, and it was going to make me finish before I could even get a crack at my beautiful, naughty wife.

But then the doorbell sounded — loud — and shocked us out of our sexual frenzy.

"*Jesus, who is that?*" Katie whispered, standing up and straightening herself out.

"I don't know," I said, hurriedly stuffing my hard, wet cock back inside my pants.

"Somebody forgot something?"

"One of our neighbors called the police about the noise?"

"We were not that noisy..."

But the suggestion that it could have been a cop made us open the door as rapidly as we were humanly able.

Robbie was standing out on our doorstep, looking sheepish.

"Uh…" he said, scratching his head. "Look, guys, I just wanted to apologize…"

He'd thought about what he did, and then he'd come back to say sorry. He looked incredibly guilty.

Katie grabbed hold of me, looking as much like a horny wife as any wife could look at that point, and simply flashed a quick, impatient smile at Robbie. "No need to apologize," she said, then her gaze returned to me as though trying to use telepathy to entice me upstairs for more passion.

Robbie looked confused, his eyes flicking from mine to Katie's and back again.

"It's all right, man,' I said. 'Really. Bygones be bygones."

Katie giggled. Robbie was peering at both of us, and I could see him trying to figure out what was going on between us. I looked at Katie, trying to determine whether our friend might have enough evidence to know what we might have just been up to before he pressed that doorbell.

My gorgeous wife was somewhat red-faced, her brow a little shiny with perspiration and her honey-gold hair a touch damp.

"Did I interrupt something?" Robbie asked cautiously.

"Goodnight, Robbie," Katie giggled.

I smiled at him, "Don't worry, man. All is forgiven…"

Katie said, "More than forgiven…"

It was when she said this that Robbie twigged what was going on. I could see he realized. He suddenly put a hand flat on our front door so we couldn't close it.

"Wait a minute," he said.

'Yes?' Katie asked, pretending to be innocent as heck.

Robbie said slowly, "You two look as horny as newlyweds. Is this about… what happened?"

Katie and I looked at each other.

Robbie told my wife, "You can't say 'no' to me, Katie. Are you guys super horny because I *kissed* you earlier?"

I shrugged. "I know it's weird, but…"

Robbie laughed. "I never thought you guys would be into that…"

I felt an odd little jolt at that. To know that what I was feeling was a 'that'. Robbie made it sound like I had a recognized condition.

"You don't have to… say anything to anyone about this?" I said to him.

He looked me up and down. Katie looked strangely elated — as though all this meant she didn't have to lie to anyone, she didn't have to do something that made her feel guilty. And at the same time, she had this air of confidence about her — it was so sexy — that was like, why should I feel guilty about being horny for my husband?

I expected Robbie to just laugh and wish us a good night before disappearing off again.

But he stood still. Said, "Katie… could you come back with me to my hotel and sleep with me tonight?"

Katie and I both gasped.

———

Out of his sight, her hand was pressing at my crotch again; I knew she could feel how hard I was.

She looked up at me, a silent question on her face.

In many respects, it was up to me. I could have told Robbie my wife is busy tonight, sleeping with me. I could do her trick of saying sure, when she next gets an available night, she'll come to sleep with you — with the sense that she'd never have an available night because she spent them all with me. But I didn't.

I gazed into my wife's eyes, and we almost telepathically thought the same thing: *Wouldn't it be wild if we actually let this happen?*

So, after a long moment where it seemed like none of us

could remember how to speak, Katie said, "Could I… pack a few things first?"

Robbie smiled. "You wouldn't need much. Anything, really. My hotel provides all the toiletries anybody could ever need…"

Katie and I just looked at each other for another long moment. Jesus. Why was this such an incredible turn-on?

My heart was thumping so hard, I swear it was in danger of punching its way out of my chest.

I wanted this.

I could tell that Katie wanted this.

It was totally crazy.

Wasn't this what her entire 'Just Say Yes' program was all about? Trying new things. Grabbing the opportunity to shake things up. Taking risks that might lead to something better.

I said to my friend, "Have you got… protection?"

He smiled and raised a hand, a small box of condoms in his palm. "I do," he said.

Katie's eyes widened, shocked that I had actually asked my friend to use condoms while sleeping with my wife. But her hand was jammed up against my stiff manhood — she could tell how I really felt about all this. My hard-on was like a damn lie detector.

"I love you," she said, stepping away from me toward Robbie.

"I love you too." Jesus, my heart felt like it was being pulled in her direction, drawn by some kind of gravity like a bright star tugged toward a black hole.

"Okay, man," Robbie said. "I'll have her back safe in the morning."

And then I watched my wife walk down to Robbie's car, and he opened the door for her to climb in.

———

What a night.

Truthfully, I was a shivering, shaking wreck when I watched that car disappear into the suburban darkness. I had to go sit down before I fell down. I felt a weird mix of exhilaration and outright terror. I felt nauseous. I cursed my friend while maintaining a stupidly hard erection.

I wondered how anyone could take advantage of a friend like Robbie had. But at the same time, I felt elated that my sweet wife was going to sleep with him.

Why was it so strangely thrilling to face the prospect of your wife cheating on you?

Katie texted me, asking if I was sure about this. I said yes. For fuck's sake. I said it's just sex. It doesn't have to mean anything.

But it did mean something. I used the word 'sex' in my text to my wife. I was confirming beyond all doubt that I consented to her having sex with my friend.

I asked her if she was sure about this. She replied, yes.

She told me she loved me.

I told her I loved her.

I sat on our couch, jerking my ridiculously hard cock as I imagined Robbie and Katie getting to his hotel. Reaching his room. Going inside, closing the door behind them. I imagined Robbie wanting to give his new superpower a little workout.

Asking Katie to take off her clothes.

Watching my wife strip for him.

Or would they simply fall together, fighting to tear each other's clothes off in the heat of passion?

Knowing Robbie, I thought it would be more like the first scenario. Robbie sitting on the end of the bed watching her slow striptease. Asking her, once she was naked, to kneel and suck his cock.

I made myself come, thinking about my friend fucking my wife. Imagining her rolling a condom down his stiff cock, then climbing onto him, slipping the tip of his manhood in her pussy. Sitting down on his pole.

It was the weirdest erotic experience of my life.

I both wanted my wife to fuck my friend and feared it. I knew she loved me and that she'd come back to me, but at the same time, I knew it might take only a request from my friend for her to do something drastic, like divorce me. I mean, divorce was legal.

I told myself there was no way Katie would divorce me. When push came to shove, she would break her pledge before she broke her family.

This was just a night of fun.

This was just *sex*.

That was the only frame of mind in which I could get any sleep at all that night.

———

I woke up at the butt crack of dawn.

No text messages from my wife while I slept.

I wasn't annoyed like I sometimes was when I didn't know where she was or what she was doing. I hoped she'd been too busy through the night to even think about texting me.

I started cleaning up the wreckage from our July 4 party. Thankfully, our kids were going to spend the day with their grandparents, precisely to give us time to clear everything up after the celebration. Well. I was done cleaning up inside two hours — a record. The cleaning gave me something to focus on besides what Katie had been doing all night.

I was stepping out of the shower when I heard the front door open and close.

As I heard her coming up the stairs, my pulse quickened rapidly, and my manhood was thickening up rapidly under the towel I clutched about my middle.

Then, there she was, standing in the doorway.

Still wearing her little summer dress from the party.

"Hey."

"Hey. You have a good time?"

Her hair was somewhat messy, her makeup practically gone. Her beautiful skin looked a little clammy.

"It was… *wonderful*."

Her eyes looked to me with a burning question left unsaid: do you still love me?

I moved to her, took her in my arms, breathing her in, pressing my mouth to hers. She smelled gently stale — a combination of lingering smells from the party, and the unmistakable scent of sex.

"It happened then?" I asked her, deliberately making my voice sound hopeful.

"Yes," she beamed, delighted at my enthusiasm. "It happened. He fucked me. Are you happy he did?"

Her hands swept down my body, finding my hardness. Freeing it from its towel enclosure, allowing the thing to drop to the floor. My hardness was enough answer for her, as her fingers curled around my stiff shaft.

I held her head in my hands and kissed her, so deeply, pressing her back against the doorway as I sucked on her full lips, as I smelled my friend's cologne on her, as I detected his cum.

"How many times?" I asked her.

"Four," she grinned. "He kept asking for more. We hardly got any sleep at all."

I was shaking, shivering, shuddering with pure lust. I wanted her so badly, I felt like I was going to explode. She giggled and slipped out of my embrace, moving to the bed.

"He said you're a *cuckold*," Katie said to me, backing up to the mattress, climbing onto it.

"A *what*?"

"A cuckold. It means you like it when your wife sleeps

with other men." She shuffled back on the mattress a little. I leaned over to kiss her mouth some more.

Had she sucked Robbie's cock with this mouth? I could hardly believe it.

"You were talking about me, then?"

"In between… you know… *sex*…" she grinned, reaching for my face as we kissed, stroking me as though she'd only just been told how valuable I was. "I told him how horny you were because of that first time he kissed me."

"The peck on the cheek?"

"The first time he kissed me properly."

I knelt over her on the bed, slipped one of the straps of her dress off her shoulder, exposing one of her small but magnificent breasts. She wasn't wearing a bra. In fact, I got the idea she'd left her underwear in Robbie's hotel room.

"Did he say anything else about me?" I asked, sliding the other strap off her body and letting her dress slip down her chest. Her bare nipples were stiff, enticing.

"That you love me so much," she said, "that it turns you on when I get to have sex with other people."

There was something oddly comforting about being given a word to describe myself. A term to be used for what I was feeling. *Cuckold*. I knew the word; I knew it meant a husband whose wife is stolen by another man. But Katie — and Robbie — seemed to be giving me a new use of it. A more modern use. A man who is turned on by his wife's infidelity.

She brushed her hair back off her shoulder and put a hand on my head as I ducked down to take one of her stiff nipples in my mouth.

"What else did he say?" I asked her between mouthfuls.

"Mmmm…" she moaned, her magnificent chest rising and falling with deep breaths as I sucked on her breasts, tasting the faint saltiness on her soft skin, inhaling that strange earthiness of recent sex emanating from her body.

She said, "He said… I should start dating other people."

"He did?"

I did a second take. I said, "Did he ask you to?"

"Uh-huh," she giggled. We kissed. We gazed at each other with thrilled smiles spread across our faces, as though we'd just won the lottery.

It was the weirdest thing. I was so excited by the thought of my wife dating other guys.

Obviously, Katie liked the thought that she might be allowed to see other people. But there was also something in her expression that said she was thrilled this might be an adventure for both of us to enjoy.

I kissed her lips. I sucked her tongue. It seemed obscene. And yet crazy hot.

"You sucked his cock?"

She nodded. "Does it freak you out?"

I shrugged. Kissed her mouth again. A mouth that had been stuffed with another man's cock. I swear, I could taste it on her. The unfamiliar flavor of her mouth was exhilarating to me. I couldn't explain why. It just was.

"He put it inside me, too, can you believe it?" she said with a mischievous smirk.

I urged her to lie back, and I pushed up her dress, revealing her spectacularly bare sex.

"You left your underwear in his room then?" I asked her.

She giggled. "He asked me to."

I dived between her warm, firm thighs and nuzzled into the sprinkle of soft, golden fur spread over her mound. She seemed surprised at what I was doing, but she wasn't stopping me. She stared down at me as though fascinated, perhaps even waiting for me to be disgusted by the stark reality that another man had shoved his dick inside her pussy.

But strangely, that thought only drove me on. Only made me hunger for her and her well-used pussy.

I opened my mouth and slid my tongue in between her

hot, rosy-red labia, my tastebuds tingling with the tangy sharpness of her come. Maybe not only her come. She was so wet, but she didn't taste the way I knew from before.

"He used a condom?" I asked her.

"Uh-huh," she said, moaning at the sensation of my mouth on her sex, but gazing down at me with wide eyes and wider mouth, stunned that I would want to lick her pussy after another man had taken her there.

It was a deviant kind of thing to do, I could see that. But I wanted it.

I wanted to feast on her unholy flesh.

I wanted to ravish her adulterous sex.

I settled between her legs and made it my home. I pressed my face to her pussy, my nose wedged in the soft fur on her mound and lapped at her copious wetness. She writhed under me, sighing and moaning at the sensations I provoked in her.

I never spent this long going down on her before. Not even close.

I was obsessed.

Practice makes perfect, too. The longer I was down there, savoring her wicked flavor, coating my entire face in her dew, the better my technique became, and the more she responded to my tongue, my lips, my fingers.

"Oh God… how can you do that?" she asked at one point.

I think she was relieved that I wasn't angry. That I hadn't turned into a rabid monster. That I hadn't refused her entry to our house.

Relief translated into an incredible sexual eagerness. An impressive sexual responsiveness.

I'd never made her come before through foreplay alone, but now she was shaking and shivering and crying out under me, and it was clear she was headed for a big win.

But she sat up and urged me over onto my back, trying to turn the focus onto me — whether because she felt guilty about the pleasure, I was giving her after what she'd done, or because she thought I'd prefer her to come on my cock.

As she straddled me, however, I took hold of her hips and hauled her up to my mouth so I could feed on her some more.

She sat on my face and put her hand on my head as I gripped her highs so tightly she couldn't escape. She ground her pussy into my eager mouth and just went with it, riding my tongue, pushing her clit against my nose.

With my head wedged between her thighs, my entire world seemed filled with her adulterous pussy. This was Heaven on Earth. I'd always been attracted to Katie, but I'd never wanted her so badly as this. I'd never been so brutally turned on by her before.

By anyone, let's face it.

My friend Robbie had taken her to his bed and fucked her four times, and now she was rubbing her soaking, freshly-fucked pussy all over my face.

No one else would understand exactly what I felt at that moment.

I sucked on my wife's unfaithful sex, and she *squirted*, for God's sake. I could hardly believe it. She'd never done anything like that before. She sat on my face and came, hard, and as she cried out, and pressed her full weight down so her pussy was crushed against my open mouth, a rush of her juices came flooding all over me, drenching me down to the neck.

Breathless, she stammered, "*What... what... wh—*"

But then I was on top of her, pressing her into the mattress, lying over her, sliding my hard cock into her juicy pussy.

It wasn't long before I came, too. Adding to the mess.

Only as we lay there, side by side, still panting to recover our breaths, did I remember the whole 'yes' thing again. That Katie would do whatever I asked, because she was trying to maintain a hold on this positivity philosophy. She was adamant it was improving her life. Who was I to argue?

"Will you fuck him again?" I said, and she looked at me with raised eyebrows, because she knew I was aware how she was supposed to answer.

"Robbie?"

"Yeah, *Robbie*," I smiled. "Will you fuck him again, this time so I can watch?"

She said yes, of course.

Max Sebastian has been writing popular erotic fiction for more than two decades, and specializes in stories about couples challenging the conventional boundaries of their relationships. He is originally from London, England, but now lives with his wife and children in Connecticut, USA. For links to his books and updates on his new releases, go to MaxSebastian.net.

MOVING A FRIEND

Sean Geist

Here I am sitting on the couch in a motel room somewhere on I-70 outside Topeka, a glass of whiskey in one hand, my hard cock in the other. I've been slowly stroking myself for the last hour keeping myself on the edge of an orgasm. My wife is in the next room over, fucking my best friend. Right now, you're probably thinking I'm contemplating something drastic, like a divorce. You'd be wrong. I knew when we started this trip we might end up here. In fact, I was counting on it.

Three weeks ago…

I came home early from work, the day before my wife and I were supposed to help my buddy move. Trent and I go way back. His family lived behind mine when I was a kid. We went to the same grade school and since we both had birthdays in May, we ended up in the same homeroom class.

Ever since then, we've been close. We ended up graduating high school fifth and sixth in a class of 354. I won't tell you which of us was fifth. We took a pair of twins to the prom. That was a story I'd love to tell sometime. The Wilson sisters. Long red hair, piercing green eyes. Rumor around the school was one of the girls liked going down on guys. I don't know if it was true. Nicole, my date, only let me get to second base. Trent never told me if he got lucky, and I never asked.

We went to the same college. I graduated a year early and went on to law school. Trent was on a soccer scholarship and ended up coaching a high school girls' team. Took them to the State finals his second year.

That's why five years later he was leaving little old Cuyahoga Falls and moving to Colorado Springs to become an assistant coach for the Major League Soccer team there.

You could say Trent and I were the kind of friends who would do anything for each other. I let him borrow my car when his was in the shop. He let me and my wife, Ashley, use his family's cabin on Lake Erie. He was the guy I called when I thought my wife was going to leave me and he talked me out of some really stupid ideas. And I was the guy he asked to help him move thirteen hundred miles.

———

That's why I was coming home early that Friday, to help my wife pack for our weeklong working vacation. I would be working. She would be vacationing.

"Ashley," I called out as I set down my keys and briefcase. "I'm home."

She didn't answer but I could hear her moving around upstairs. I found her in our bedroom. She had her back to me, her brown hair up in a bun, and pink headphones covering her ears. She wore matching pink cotton shorts and a black crop top.

I felt myself stiffen. She was swaying her hips to music only she could hear, her arms moving in serpentine patterns in the air. She was supposed to be packing, but there wasn't much of that going on. And at that moment, I really didn't care.

I was mesmerized by Ashley's sexy dance, and remembering the day, a few weeks back, when I caught her kissing Trent. It was a quick peck on the cheek that turned into something a bit more passionate.

We were at dinner, the three of us, and Trent had just told us about his new job and how he'd be leaving Ohio and starting over in Colorado. I had excused myself to use the bathroom and when I came back, I saw them. I felt a warm glow in my heart when I saw my wife kiss his cheek. But when he twisted his head and their lips locked together, it was like a stab to the heart. I wanted to rush in and punch him. But I didn't. Instead, I leaned back against the wall. I took a few shallow breaths. And to my horror, I felt my cock stir.

I found it arousing to see my wife part her lips and allow another man's tongue to invade her mouth. The whole kiss lasted only a minute, but by the time they parted my cock was rock hard.

I watched my wife sit down, a look of shock on her flushed face. Trent sat next to her and took her hand in his. They started talking. I had to rush back to the bathroom and masturbate, filling a wad of toilet paper with my cum.

When I got back, they were chatting away like nothing happened. I knew better, but I didn't let them know what I saw. I wanted to keep it my secret.

The memory of that day came rushing back as I watched my wife dancing. I wanted to reach in and grab her waist, nuzzle my nose in her neck, and savage her with kisses. I wanted to pull down her shorts and panties and bury my hard cock inside her moist pussy.

But I knew if I did that, I'd scare the living shit out of her and she might not ever feel like fucking me again. So, instead,

I backed away and went back downstairs and sent her a text message.

+Greg

Love the way you dance.

A few seconds later I heard her movement stop then she shouted out, "Greg, you Fucker!" She raced down the stairs to jump into my arms. "Have you been watching me?"

I kissed her on the mouth and set her down. "Only for a little while. I came home early to help you pack. And it's a good thing I did."

Ashley gave me a thump on the chest. "You calling me lazy?"

"I'm saying Trent wants us over at his place by seven in the morning. Most of his stuff has been loaded in his rental van, but he said there's a few more things to pack in our Wrangler. He wants to be on the road by eight."

"Hey, babe. Relax," my wife said as she pulled me upstairs. "I've already got my stuff packed." She pointed at her suitcase in the hall; I totally missed it earlier. "I've got the Yeti stuffed with snacks and drinks, and our tablets and phones are fully charged."

She slid the half-empty suitcase onto the floor and pushed me down on the bed.

Then she lifted her black top, letting her modest breasts free.

"I've got everything under control," she said as she unzipped my pants and pulled out my cock. "Now, let me get this trip off to a good start with a blow job. You like the sound of that?"

I nodded my head while I untied my tie and took off my shirt.

I was nearly knocked out when she took my erection into her warm mouth. She bobbed her head a few times and licked the length of my shaft.

"You like that?"

"You know it."

"You're going to return the favor, right?"

"Oh, fuck yeah," I said.

This trip had shifted our libidos into overdrive, and I was pretty sure I knew why. I was still aroused at the thought of my wife getting frisky with another man, and I had a sneaky suspicion she was still hot from the kiss.

It'd been gloriously insane. Two weeks of sucking and fucking almost every night. We even had anal for the first time. It was magical.

I very much wanted this carnal energy to continue on our trip and planned to do everything in my power to make that happen.

———

It only took us about fifteen minutes to put the last of Trent's belongings in our Jeep Wrangler, so we were on the road a half hour earlier than expected. After topping off the tanks, we stopped at IHOP to top off our stomachs.

Ashley and I sat on one side of the booth, Trent on the other. The faux leather seat was sticky with syrup, but we didn't care. We were three friends having a final adventure together.

"You have any trouble with the landlord?" Ashley asked. "Breaking the lease, and all."

Trent took a sip of coffee. "Nah, the team covered the last two months of rent and the cleaning deposit."

"And they even found you a new place in Colorado Springs?" I asked.

"Yeah. But I think I'm going to try to find a house."

"Oh, paying you the big bucks now, I see," Ashley said.

Trent laughed. "It's enough. I'm tired of renting."

"You won't say that the first time your water heater bursts in the middle of the night."

We all laughed, then continued chatting until our food arrived. The food was mediocre, and the coffee sucked, but we needed fuel and it would do. We ate and talked. Trent paid the bill, and we were back on the road.

———

Before the trip Ashley and I created a playlist that would last us the entire twenty-hour drive without any repeats. We didn't talk much early on. Ashley read a book on her tablet, and I tried my best to keep up with Trent in his van.

In the absence of conversation, I had plenty of time to think. And all I could think about was my wife and my buddy. In the seven years that Ashley has been in my life, never once did I notice any sign of physical attraction between the two. And it's not like there hadn't been a lot of chances. All the times the three of us have been together at the lake, my wife wearing a skimpy bikini and laying out in the sun, I don't remember ever catching Trent giving her more than a quick glance.

Of course, that might be because I was too busy staring myself. And Ashley isn't shy about walking around the cabin we shared in her underwear or even just a towel. We've been three friends, having casual fun, and never once did I imagine things taking a sexual turn.

That was until I saw the kiss, and my eyes were opened. Now all I could think about was how long the two of them have been harboring these feelings of desire. Have they ever kissed before that? I didn't think so. What I saw that day was a passionate first kiss. I think it surprised all three of us.

I stole a quick glance at Ashley. Her attention was focused on her book. And all of a sudden, I was wondering if she would be simply reading if she was riding with Trent. Instead of focusing on her tablet, would she focus on our friend?

What would they chat about? Would the passions that flared that evening two weeks ago reignite?

I felt my cock stir as I thought about my wife, alone with Trent, free to explore their new-found feelings.

The idea scared and thrilled me, and I decided to throw caution to the wind and let it happen.

We were approaching Dayton when Trent pulled off and turned into a fast food joint for lunch. This was my chance.

"Hey, Ash, I was thinking," I said as we pulled off the highway.

"Yeah?" My wife was putting her tablet away and slipping her shoes back on.

"I wonder how Trent is doing, driving alone."

"What are you getting at?" Ashley looked at me with questioning eyes.

"Maybe, after lunch, you should ride with him. Keep him company."

"Greg, are you trying to get rid of me?"

"Don't be silly. I just think you and Trent should spend a little time together. Now that he's living in Colorado, we're not going to see him as often."

I don't know what I thought my wife would say, but I was surprised when she didn't argue and quickly agreed to ride with Trent for the rest of the day's drive.

———

After a quick meal Trent and I swapped places. I would drive the moving van and he would ride in the Wrangler. Ashley offered to drive, but Trent said no, he didn't like being a passenger.

So, after a quick exchange of keys, we were off again.

I left my phone with our music playlist with Ashley, so I tried to find something on the radio to keep my mind occupied. Unfortunately, there was nothing to listen to other than county stations and talk radio, so I chose to make the drive in silence.

Every so often I'd glance in the side mirrors and see what my wife and Trent were up to. Again, I don't know what I expected to see, but every time I looked, they were just chatting and driving.

I felt a little jealous. When she drove with me, she just read her book, but now, my buddy was the focus of her attention. Of course that was the whole reason for switching places, letting them spend a few hours together before our friendship inevitably faded away.

They were making great use of the time. Every time I looked, one of them was talking, while the other listened or laughed. Once, I caught Ashley reaching over and it looked like she put her hand on Trent's knee. It was an innocent gesture, but it still made my cock twitch.

"God, Greg, what are you doing?" I asked myself out loud.

I didn't have an answer, or at least a good one. I was practically throwing my wife at another man. Yes, Ashley made the first move, when she kissed him, but that was all she did, at least as far as I knew. I had no reason to think she ever cheated on me.

Imagining the sexual tension between my wife and my best friend had me hard as a rock. It was crazy, but true. And by the time we arrived at our planned stop for the evening, at a motel near St. Louis, I had convinced myself that I wanted my wife to sleep with Trent. I knew they liked each other but she would never break our vows. So, it would be up to me to make it happen.

———

"I saw you kiss him," I said as we lay in bed. I had just turned out the lights and Ashley had set aside her tablet.

"What do you mean? We just talked and listened to music."

"Not today. A couple of weeks ago. At dinner."

My wife didn't have a quick answer. Her silence lasted a few moments but was soon broken by the sound of sobs.

"No, don't cry. Please," I said. This was not going the way I wanted.

"I'm sorry, Greg, I really am. I should have—I should have told you. I thought. It was."

I put my arm around my wife, and she clung to me.

"Will you stop it? I'm not mad."

Ashley suddenly stopped crying. "You're not?"

"No."

"Why not?"

"I don't know. I should be, right? But I'm not. In fact..." I paused. How do you tell your wife you want to watch her fuck another man? It's not something one does.

"In fact, what?"

I didn't know what to say, so I decided to turn the tables. "Tell me."

"Tell you what?"

"Tell me."

I didn't say more. I would leave it up to Ashley.

"You'll get mad," she eventually said. "I know it."

"I swear. Nothing you tell me tonight will make me mad."

Ashley squinted, like she doubted me.

"Cross my heart. You can tell me anything and I won't get mad."

"What if… What if I told you that you had bad breath?"

I breathed into my palm and smelled. "Do I?"

My wife gave me a playful smack in the chest. "No stupid. I was making a hypothetical."

"Then I would use some mouthwash, but I wouldn't get mad."

"What if I said you were a lousy lover?"

That one hurt, even though I knew it wasn't true. I didn't answer right away.

"Hah! See. You're mad."

"Ashley, are you saying I'm a bad lover?"

My wife paused for a moment, but eventually she said, "Of course not. I'm just checking."

"Just tell me."

The dark motel room was filled with silence again, broken only by the sound of passing traffic on the freeway and the occasional heavy footstep on the ceiling. Eventually, Ashley spilled her story.

"Ever since you introduced me to Trent, I've thought he was hot. And his body, shit, Greg, it's beautiful, and he keeps it up, working out the way he does. I've watched him work out, a couple of times, and got so horny. You want to know when? Think back to the nights I dragged you to the bedroom for a quickie as soon as you got home. Yeah, those were the days I watched him.

"You said you wouldn't get mad. Oh, you like that? You like me telling you how hot I think your best friend is? Your cock seems to agree. You're dripping from the tip. So anyway, that night at the restaurant, I let my emotions take over and I kissed him. Yes, I made the first move, but you saw that. No, I never cheated on you. Yes, I thought of him once or twice when I masturbated. Okay, a few more times than that.

"Honey, I'm sorry. You wanted the truth. Why are you looking at me like that? Greg? Greg?"

As I listened to my wife explain her attraction to another man, my cock got harder and harder. The words stung my heart but aroused me in ways I can't explain. I'd heard enough. I rolled over onto Ashley.

"Spread your legs," I said, making my voice as commanding as I could. I never ordered my wife to do anything. I'm not that stupid. But tonight, I felt the need to establish my dominance. And it worked. Ashley spread her legs and I settled between them. My hard cock nestled at the entrance to her pussy.

"Fuck, you're wet," I said. "Thinking about Trent?"

"Fuck you, Greg," my wife said as she grabbed my ass and pulled me deep inside her. "You're the one getting hard listening to me tell you how hot your best friend is. You should be mad, not horny."

"Don't. Tell. Me. What. To. Do." I started fucking my wife, thrusting with each word, as hard as I could.

"Harder, Greg. Harder."

I sped up my thrusts. I felt a deep need to show my wife just how good I could fuck. For some reason, I needed to show her I was better than Trent.

"Oh, yes, Greg. So good."

I could feel her body begin to tremble. "Take my cock, you slut. Take it."

"Ohhhhhhhhhh, fuuuuuuck."

I had to cover my wife's mouth with my hand as her orgasm overtook her. I didn't want anyone calling the cops on us. I felt the walls of her pussy clench around my shaft, and I quickly came. "Take my cum, Ash. Take it all."

I pushed myself as deep as I could and I released, filling my wife's womb with my seed.

It took us a moment to catch our breath. Neither of us wanted to discuss what the fuck had happened. We were too tired from the long drive and the rough fucking.

Ashley went to the bathroom to clean up. I was asleep by the time she got back to bed.

———

We had breakfast the next morning at a Denny's next to the motel. Trent was already there when we arrived.

"You guys really made a racket last night," he said as soon

as the waitress was out of earshot. "You guys fuck like that all the time?"

We answered simultaneously.

"Yes."

"I wish."

Trent laughed. We finished breakfast and got three coffees to go. Trent took the van. Ashley and I took the Wrangler. She drove.

"I'm sorry I called you a slut last night," I said, somewhere about halfway to Kansas City.

Ashley laughed. "It was kind of hot."

"You think so?"

"Yeah. I was being a slut, telling you how hot I think your friend is."

"He's our friend, isn't he?"

She thought for a moment before answering. "Yeah. I guess, but he's not one with benefits."

I think she was lying a bit. She told me she masturbated thinking about him. I liked to rub one out thinking about Jennifer Lawrence, but I never thought I'd ever fuck her. My wife saw Trent at least once or twice a week.

"So, you never cheated?"

"No, never. Just that kiss."

"That's not cheating, Ash."

"Some would say it was."

"I'm not some."

"I know. You fucked me pretty hard. You thinking about me and your buddy right now?"

"Yes, honestly. It's pretty hot thinking of you two together."

My wife drove in silence for a bit more. I tried to go back to reading while we listened to our playlist, but I kept thinking about the two of them fucking, and how much I wanted it to happen. I was on dangerous ground and would have to tread lightly.

"Honey, you say you never cheated, and I believe you. But have you ever thought about it?"

"Cheating? No."

"Really? Not with Trent?"

She didn't answer.

"You can tell me."

"I told you I fantasized about him. His hot, sweaty body. But that's all."

"You never thought about him fucking you? Impaling you on his thick cock? Thrusting himself deep inside you while sucking on your breasts?"

"You better stop that, Greg."

"Getting you wet?"

"Yeah. And I have to concentrate on driving."

I was glad to see she wasn't getting mad at me, and I took that as a sign it was safe to make my final suggestion.

"Would you like to fuck him?"

The question hung heavy in the air between us. Ashley didn't say anything, and I thought she might not have heard me. I was about to ask again when she finally spoke up.

"I'm not sure how to answer that, Greg."

"Yes or no would suffice."

"Why are you asking?"

I didn't know how to answer that, so I guess we were even. I could tell her I didn't know, but I did. The reason I asked was because I wanted her to fuck him. What I didn't know was why I wanted that. Why did I get hard and horny thinking about her cheating on me with my best friend?

"Honey, you still with me?" Ashley asked.

"Yeah. I just. I want to know. Because—because I want you to do it. I want you to fuck him."

"Are you crazy?"

"No, hear me out. Ever since I saw you kiss him, I've been having dark thoughts of you two together and I get aroused."

"That's why you fucked me so hard last night, thinking about me fucking him."

"Yeah. It made me jealous and angry and fuck I've never felt anything like it."

"And you enjoy that feeling, of jealousy?"

"Yeah. I don't know why, but I do."

"And you think you'd enjoy it more if I actually fucked him?"

"Yes. I do."

My wife stopped talking and spent the next hour thinking about what I said. I tried to read but couldn't. My mind was distracted by the question that hung between us. When Trent signaled he was exiting the freeway for our lunch stop, my wife finally spoke.

"I won't say I would hate sleeping with Trent because I wouldn't. But I'm afraid you'd hate me after I did it."

"Never, Ash. I'd never hate you."

"You can't know that. And after we've done it, there would be no going back. You can't unfuck someone."

I could feel my excitement waning, quickly replaced by a sense of disappointment.

"So, you're saying you won't do it?"

Ashley sighed. "I don't think I should. Not because I don't want to. It's that I care about you more than I care about my desire to fuck your friend. That's a fantasy. What we have is real."

"But if I gave you my permission. How—"

"You say that now. But what if I actually do it and you don't enjoy it? No. I need to be sure this is what you want."

"What are you saying, Ash?"

"I'm saying I need proof that sleeping with Trent won't end our marriage."

"What proof is that?"

My cock was hard when I started our conversation, but

when I thought my wife was going to decline my offer, it had started to deflate.

"After lunch, you're going to switch vehicles again. You drive the van and Trent will drive the Wrangler. I will be with him. And I'll blow him."

I caught my breath and my cock got hard.

"And if you still love me, and cherish me, after I do that, then I know you'll be fine if I fuck him. But if your jealousy is more excruciating than you can stand, this goes no further. And you have to live with the fact you let your wife suck another man's cock while you watched."

By the time she was finished, my cock was hard as steel again. Ashley snickered when she saw me adjust myself.

"I think this will work out fine," she said as she followed Trent's van into the restaurant parking lot.

———

Trent had no problems with switching vehicles again. We finished lunch and my buddy made sure I knew where the hotel was. We had another four-hour drive ahead of us, so we wasted no time getting back on the road.

My wife gave me a kiss on the cheek and whispered into my ear. "I'll text you when I'm about to make my move. Don't get into an accident."

We were about an hour into the afternoon's drive when my phone buzzed. The notification popped up over the map App on my phone.

+Ashley

I hope you enjoy this as much as I will

I was following the Wrangler and saw my wife wave at me. I waved back, then she turned to Trent and started chatting.

How I wished I could hear what they were saying. For his part, my buddy kept his eyes on the road, but every so often I noticed him glance to the side and give my wife a questioning look. Once he even met my gaze in the rearview mirror.

He shook his head. My wife kept talking. Trent shrugged his shoulders and looked back at me following again.

Ashley reached over to Trent's lap. I assumed she was taking out his cock. My penis grew hard as I watched my wife's arms move in a rhythmic motion. I could tell she was stroking him. Her eyes grew wide, and I could only assume his cock was growing larger than she expected. After a short while, she gave me one last look and disappeared behind the seat, her head moving toward Trent's lap.

I adjusted myself as I watched her blow my buddy. My steely cock strained against the confines of my khaki shorts. Trent kept his eyes on the road. I'm glad he didn't try to glance back at me as I watched my wife service him.

My phone buzzed. I glanced over at it in its dashboard holder. My wife had texted me a picture. I tapped the thumbnail and up popped a picture of my wife licking a drop of clear liquid from the tip of a very large cock.

Her fingers were barely able to reach all the way around the shaft. I had to fight the urge to rub myself through my shorts. Seeing my wife worshiping another man's erection should have made me sick, but instead it aroused me. I was jealous and mad, yes, but I was enjoying the buzz it created in my gut.

I looked back at the road. Nothing had changed. Trent still looked straight ahead, but he was reaching over and playing with Ashley's ass. As I watched, my buddy started to squirm. He ran the fingers of his free hand through his short black hair. Suddenly, Trent gripped the wheel with both hands and tensed up. He must have been cumming, most likely filling my wife's throat with semen.

A menagerie of raging feelings played in my brain. Lust and desire danced with jealousy and anger. Worry and shame joined with pride and glee in a sensual orgy of emotions. If I had so much as touched my cock, I'm sure I would have erupted in my pants.

My reaction to seeing my wife go down on another man scared me. Maybe I was enjoying it too much? Fuck it, who cares. This was my life—our life. If Ashley wanted to play with someone else, why should I be bothered, especially when it filled me with delicious angst? Watching my wife go down on Trent had revealed a hidden kink. I didn't know what this discovery meant for the future of our marriage, but one thing I was sure of, I wanted to explore it to its bitter end. And that meant letting her actually fuck him.

———

Trent didn't say anything to me when we arrived at the hotel. He checked us in and handed me our room key without looking me in the eyes.

"We should leave here around eight if we want to get to Colorado Springs at a decent hour."

It was obvious Trent felt bad for letting my wife suck his cock while I was in the other car, but instead of apologizing, he tried to pretend it didn't happen. His reaction bothered me. Not because of what my wife did with him, but the way he was acting after the fact. Like he was mad at me or thought I might be mad at him. I couldn't let this wound fester and grow into something that could destroy our friendship.

I gave Ashley a look. She could tell I needed a little alone time with Trent. It is a subtle skill couples learn that lets them communicate without words.

"I'm heading to the room," she said.

"I'll be there in a minute," I told her and kissed her on the cheek.

"I think I need to—" Trent started.

"Hold on buddy." I grabbed my friend's arm. He stiffened up like he was ready for a punch. "Relax, dude."

I let go of Trent.

"Hey, Greg, look. I'm sorry."

"It's cool, Trent, really it is."

He gave me a weird look. I pulled him away from the check-in desk and we sat down to talk. I explained that Ashley told me what she was going to do, and I gave her my blessing.

"Consider it a little going away gift, from Ashley and myself."

"You do this for all your friends?" Trent asked. His little joke released some of the tension that had been hanging between us.

"No. Just the best ones," I said.

"So, we're good?"

"Absolutely," I said.

I got up to go, but now it was Trent's turn to keep the conversation going.

"You're a lucky man, Greg, to have a wife like Ash."

"I know man. I am. And I don't mind sharing."

I gave Trent a handshake and a hug and went to my room.

———

I closed the door behind me and was attacked by my wife. She jumped into my arms and gave me a hard, passionate kiss. Our tongues swirled together in a tango of desire. Her breath tasted minty.

"Glad you washed your mouth out," I said when we finally separated.

"You think I'd want you to taste a little of Trent on my breath?"

"I don't know. Sounds kinky."

I started tickling Ashley. She squirmed in my grasp, and we fell onto the bed, rolling around like horny teenagers.

All afternoon, I wanted nothing more than to take my wife

and fuck her silly. But I couldn't do that yet. There was one more thing I wanted her to do first.

"I think you should go to Trent's room and spend the night," I said.

Ashley leaned up on her elbows and gave me a questioning look. "Are you sure? You really want me to do this?"

I grabbed her hand and placed it against my erection. Even through my shorts, I'm sure she could feel my pulse.

"Yes. I do. Watching you suck his dick was amazing. It hurt and stung but also aroused and excited me. I want to feel that again."

"And you'll still want to remain married to my cheating ass?"

Ashley stood up and looked down at me, her eyes scanning my face for any hint of doubt.

"Ash, it's a cute ass, and it's not cheating if I let you do it, and yes I'll still want to be married to it. Now run and give Trent the fucking of his life, before I change my mind and fuck you myself."

Ashley paused, like she was thinking about taking me up on the offer. I grabbed a pillow and threw it at her. She squealed and laughed and left me alone with my angst and my raging hard-on.

That's how I ended up lying in bed naked, slowly stroking myself. My eyes are closed and I'm imagining Ashley and Trent in bed. His body is wedged between her open thighs. He's thrusting his hips, driving his cock into her wet pussy.

I see her arms wrapped around his back. She's digging her nails into his bare skin as wave after wave of pleasure rolls through her body.

She's moaning his name.

"Yes, Trent, that feels so good. Fuck me."

He doesn't say anything. He speeds up his thrusts. He grabs her ass and pushes deep. Then he holds himself still and with a growl he comes.

"Yes. Oh God, yes! Give me your cum. Fill me up, Trent."

I have to stop stroking or I'll cum myself, and I need to be ready to reclaim my wife when she returns.

Now…

It's been almost two hours now. I told her to spend the night, but now I want her back. I feel a need growing within me. A desire to roughly take my wife. Fuck her hard. Remind her that I'm her husband.

I feel a mix of anger and jealousy again, more than I felt earlier when I watched her blow him. It's an angst that feels like an ice pick in my heart, a punch in the gut, and a kick in my balls. And I'm loving every minute of it.

It's two am when she returns. I hear her key in the door. The lights are out, but I can see her move across the room in silhouette.

She yelps when I grab her.

"Greg? Honey?"

I kiss her hard. She melts in my grasp. This time I can taste him. His salty cum on her breath. She didn't have time to clean herself. Good. I want to take her like the dirty slut she is.

I throw her down on the bed.

"Did he come inside you?" I ask as I pull her jeans and panties off in one fell swoop.

"Yes, he did." Ashley pulls her shirt off, ripping buttons as she goes. She's as eager as I am. "Twice."

"Fuck! You dirty whore."

I crawl onto the bed and mount her. Her pussy is drenched, I can't tell if it's her juices or his semen. Probably a bit of both.

"Did you enjoy it? Fucking Trent?"

"Oh, hell yes. His cock is so big. He really stretched me out."

"How many times did you come?"

"I don't know—three, four times."

"You're so wet. Can you even feel me?"

"Yes, Greg. I can feel you. Why are you asking so many questions? Shut up and fuck me."

I want this feeling to last forever. My cock buried in Ashley's warm, moist pussy, my arms wrapped around her, our naked bodies pressing against each other.

Unfortunately, I've been on edge all night and I erupt after a few more thrusts, adding my load to Trent's. I flex my cock, making sure she takes every drop.

When I'm done, I roll over and give a loud sigh of relief.

"Fuck, that was amazing," I say.

"It was."

We lie back and just breathe for a bit. I close my eyes and feel the angst ebb from my body. I reach over and squeeze my wife's hand.

"I love you, Ash."

"I love you too, Greg."

I want to talk, but we're both too tired and we quickly fall asleep.

———

I wake up to the wonderful sensation of my wife's lips wrapped around my cock.

"Morning, sleepy head," she says as she slides up my body and impales herself on my erection. "Oh shit, that feels good."

She leans down and kisses me as she rolls her hips.

"Good, you brushed your teeth."

She slaps my chest. "You loved it last night. When you attacked me before I could take a shower and clean up."

"I'm sorry. An urge came over me, and I had to have you. The dirtier the better. Like I needed proof of your infidelity."

"Remember, it wasn't cheating."

"I know. But what else can I call it?"

"Who cares? Fuck your wife."

"My cheating wife." I laugh.

"Yeah, your cheating, whore wife."

I roll us over and give Ashley a good hard fucking. I last a little longer than the previous night. I think I might have even given her an orgasm.

We quickly shower and get ready to head out.

I don't know exactly how this encounter is going to change our relationship with Trent or our marriage. Will she fuck him again when we get to Colorado? Will she want to stay and help him get settled while I drive back to Ohio? And are there any other guys back home that we might want her to play with?

There are so many questions I don't have the answers to, yet. But we still have an eight-hour drive ahead of us today. Plenty of time to work it out.

Sean Geist has been writing filthy stories for almost a decade. He writes about wives who love to break their wedding vows in a variety of ways. Sometimes the husbands encourage this behavior, but often they end up getting dragged along for the ride. Either way, everyone ends up satisfied. Sean can sometimes be found on Twitter (@seangeist) or more often on Medium (@seangeist). You can also reach him at seangeist@outlook.com.

THE REMAKE

Paul Garland

As the gentle hum and rhythmic bubbling of the hot tub filled the air, a sanctuary from the world back home, Isla's gaze lingered a moment too long on a passing member of the spa staff. The flicker of recognition, or perhaps something more, didn't escape me. When her eyes finally met mine, there was an unspoken question hanging between us, made heavier in the steam and serenity of our secluded hotel retreat.

"Did you hear anything of what I just said?" I asked, quirking my lips into an amused smile.

"I'm sorry," my wife started, a faint blush colouring her cheeks, a rare occurrence that told me this was no ordinary moment. "He just... he reminded me of someone."

"And who might that be?" I probed, curiosity laced with a hint of amusement. It was unlike Isla to get so distracted, especially in a moment as serene as this.

"Oh, no one important," she said, the words coming out almost like a sigh, laden with fake nonchalance. "Just a guy I used to know."

I watched as her green eyes flickered to the same man as he walked past again, this time in the opposite direction, a tray filled with cocktails in hand. Unconsciously, she took hold of a stray strand of her long red hair, twirling it around her fingers for a moment.

"No one, huh?"

Her eyes snapped back to me, the pinkness of her cheeks deepening. "Ah, yeah. Sorry, he just looks like him a lot."

"Looks like who a lot?" I wasn't giving up on finding out who the doppelganger reminded her of so much as to distract her like this.

"Alex," she sighed again, then when she realised how that sounded, she cleared her throat. "Anyway, you were talking about something. Tell me again. I'll listen properly this time."

"Alex?" I echoed, drawing the connection with a thread of realisation. "Your ex, Alex? The one you—" I trailed off, leaving the sentence to hang in the humid air, a bridge to the past she rarely spoke of.

"Yes, that Alex," she confirmed, her eyes now fixed on the rippling water, as if it could hide her from the weight of the confession. "Let's forget about him. Talk to me."

"It doesn't matter," I replied, shaking my head. Isla and I had been married for over ten years, together five years longer than that. She'd had several ex-boyfriends before we met but she rarely talked about any of them apart from Alex. "It wasn't anything important. Perhaps we should talk about Alex instead."

"You like me telling you about him, don't you?" Isla's green eyes wrinkled at the corners when she smiled. I loved that about her. "Because he was the one that I was most naughty with."

"I'm just curious," I shrugged, sitting upright in the warm, bubbling water so I could grab my beer from the edge. "What was it about him that brought you out of yourself?"

Isla had told me that she was quite shy and reserved with most of her boyfriends until she met Alex, but she'd never completely explained why. I looked at the hotel staff member as he continued to serve drinks to the people in the other hot tub, a way across the spa's luxurious garden retreat. He wasn't anything extraordinary to look at. Tall, sure, dark-haired, but not outlandishly good-looking or particularly well-built or athletic.

Isla leaned back, the bubbling water of the hot tub framing her like a mermaid in her element, her red hair fanning out in the water. She caught my gaze, her green eyes sparkling with a mix of mischief and reminiscence. "Alex was... different," she began, her voice carrying a new warmth, as if the very mention of his name brought back a flush of those old feelings. "He had a way of making me feel seen, you know? It was as if he noticed the parts of me I'd kept hidden, even from myself."

I sipped my beer, my curiosity piqued, watching her closely. "Seen how? What made him so different in the bedroom?" I found myself asking the question before I could weigh it.

She chuckled, a sound that mixed well with the symphony of the spa. "It wasn't just about the bedroom, Ethan. It was... everything. He encouraged me to be bolder, to speak my mind, to chase after what I wanted without apology." She paused, her gaze drifting off to the steam rising into the night air. "And yes, that confidence spilled over into... our more intimate moments."

"Go on," I encouraged, setting my beer aside. This was a side of Isla I'd glimpsed but never fully understood, and now, I was being invited into this private room of her past.

"In the bedroom, he was adventurous, always suggesting new things to try, things I hadn't even thought about. And he always made sure I was okay with it," she continued, her cheeks flushing with the heat of the water—or perhaps the conversation. "It made me trust him, made me feel like I could let go and just... be."

"And that was exciting for you?" I asked, trying to keep

my tone neutral, intrigued by the revelations unfolding between us.

"Immensely," she replied, locking eyes with me and winking. "You know, you should be grateful to him."

"Oh?" I smiled at her teasing. "Because he taught you everything you know… all your bedroom skills?"

"Yes," she giggled, then continued, her tone more serious. "But besides that, he made me into the more confident woman you fell in love with."

"I guess." I nodded, picking up my bottle and taking a long drink of the refreshing cool beer as the hotel staff member walked past yet again. I waved the drink at him in salute, causing him to take a step backwards. "Thanks, Mister Alex Lookalike."

"Um," he looked at me warily, confusion in his eyes. "You're welcome."

Isla laughed out loud as the young man moved on and then our conversation turned back to the innocuous subject I'd been trying to get her interested in before she became so distracted.

———

Lying in the soft embrace of our hotel bed, the crisp sheets a cool contrast to the warmth of our skin, the night whispered through the slightly ajar balcony door, carrying with it the scent of the spa's flowering gardens. The room was dim, lit only by the moon's silver glow filtering through the sheer curtains, casting ethereal patterns across the bed. Isla, nestled against me, her head on my chest, seemed content in the silence, a stark contrast to the earlier bubbling conversations in the hot tub.

Yet, the name that had surfaced earlier, Alex, lingered in my mind like the aftertaste of a strong spirit, piquing my curiosity further. Despite the tranquil setting, a part of me couldn't let go of the thread we'd pulled at earlier. "So, Isla," I began, my voice low in the quiet room, "Going back to Alex..."

She tensed slightly, her reluctance palpable. "Ethan, do we have to talk about him again?" Her voice was a mix of weariness and caution as if revisiting the topic might disturb the peace we'd found.

"I don't mean to pry," I said, tracing patterns on her back with my fingers, hoping to ease her tension. "It's just... you know I sometimes like talking about—"

"About the sex we had. Yes, I know," she interrupted me. She sighed, going silent for a moment, her breath steady against my skin. Shifting, she propped herself up on one elbow, her eyes searching mine in the moonlight drifting in through the hotel room window. "What do you want to know?"

"Tell me about the time at his parents' house," I ventured after a moment's thought. "The risky night you mentioned once but never elaborated on. You said it was crazy hot."

Isla paused, a smile playing at the corners of her lips, the moonlight accentuating her features. "It was crazy hot. It was also reckless." Her voice was a whisper, as if sharing a secret meant for only the two of us. "His parents were asleep upstairs, and the thrill of getting caught added an edge to everything. We were in the living room, on the couch that squeaked with every movement, so we ended up fucking on the floor. We had to be quiet, so quiet, but it was hard, almost impossible with the intensity between us."

"Was this at the start of your relationship?" I asked, my cock stirring at the thought of Isla, younger and less experienced, fooling around at her boyfriend's parents' house.

"We were only together for two years," Isla reminded me. "This was early on, yeah, so I'd have been nineteen, maybe twenty."

"So why was it crazy hot?" I slid a hand beneath the

sheets, finding my cock and stroking it as I always did when she told me a story from her past.

"Because it was so risky. Alex stripped me totally naked and fucked me on the floor, hard and fast and deep." Isla shifted in bed, her hand sliding over my chest towards where my hand was toying with myself. "We weren't under any covers. If his father had come downstairs at any moment and turned the light on, he'd have seen everything."

"Wow," I breathed, feeling her hand replace mine, working my stiff cock slowly.

"He recorded it too. Not our first sex tape but certainly the riskiest one. Alex had set up his camera without telling me at first. It was on a shelf, discreet, but when I noticed, I didn't stop him. It felt daring, and exciting to be filmed, knowing we could be discovered at any moment. That's why I came so hard with him that night."

The way she recounted the story, her eyes alight with the memory, fired me up even more, igniting something within me as it always did. It wasn't jealousy, but rather an intrigue, a deepening of desire for the woman beside me, who had such wildness in her when she was younger.

"That and because of his big cock," I surmised, something that she'd told me about before.

"Well, there is that," she giggled, her hand working my dick faster. "But I like your average one more. You know that right?"

"Sure you do. Anyway, how many sex tapes did you end up making?" I found myself asking, my voice rough with burgeoning arousal, imagining the scenes she described.

"Five or six," she replied, her gaze locking with mine, a hint of mischief there. "But as I told you, they all got deleted when we broke up. I made him do it. A closing of that chapter."

The idea of those tapes—now lost—was tantalizing, yet

the knowledge that she shared this part of herself with me, in words, in trust, was infinitely more intimate.

"I wish I could have seen them," I sighed, then groaned as her hand squeezed around my cock, tugging it slowly but more firmly.

"Oh, really?" Isla asked, her voice amused. "You'd like to watch the younger me getting fucked, would you?"

"Hell yeah," I replied.

"What would you like to see in particular?" Isla let go of my cock, pushing back the covers and sitting up.

"Everything," I confessed, enjoying the sight of her as she stripped off the T-shirt she was wearing to reveal she had nothing beneath. "Your pussy taking a big cock. You sucking it."

"I struggled to get my mouth around it," she murmured sexily, her hands caressing her small but soft breasts, her fingers finding her small nipples and stroking them for a moment while considering me. "He liked to grab my hair and force my head down until I gagged."

"That's horny," I encouraged her. "Keep going."

Isla let one hand slide from her breasts, gliding over her stomach to between her legs, where she stroked her pussy, her mound sparsely covered in fine reddish hair.

"One of the best videos we made," she continued, "Had him fucking my throat until he came. He pulled out and finished all over my face. I thought it was gross at the time but when I think about it now, it's really fucking horny."

"That sounds fucking amazing," I sighed. I couldn't take my eyes off her as she slid a finger inside herself.

"It was, I guess," she moaned, fingering herself with two fingers, her eyes locking onto mine and holding them. "But I enjoyed having it cum inside me. The feeling of his big, strong, hard dick shooting his load deep in my pussy…"

"I'd love to have seen that," I said, wanking myself off now while watching her grind herself onto her fingers. "I can't help but wonder what your face looked like as you got pounded by him."

"And the noises I made when I came on his cock?"

"Yes," I admitted, smiling as she finally threw a leg over me, positioning my cock at the entrance to her pussy.

"You know," she whispered, as she sank onto me, the feeling of her tight wetness around my hard cock exquisite as it always was. "I wish I still had the videos too. We could watch them together. Get horny together and have really dirty, turned-on sex like this."

"I wish," I agreed softly, taking hold of her hips, and guiding her as she began to ride me. "That would be a dream. Watching the old videos of my slutty young wife get fucked hard."

"I *was* slutty," she giggled, then went silent as she rocked on me hard and fast while rubbing her clit. "He brought that slutty side of me out like no one else could."

"I bet he enjoyed every fucking moment," I said, several minutes later, after we'd both come. I'd finished first, shooting my load deep inside her. Isla had finished moments later, grinding herself onto me while teasing her clit with her fingertips. Now we were lying in bed, both naked, the sheets tangled around our sweat-covered bodies. "I wonder if he still thinks about it, like you do."

"You're really that curious, huh?" she murmured. "Maybe you should ask him."

"How am I going to do that?" I chuckled.

"He's on my Facebook."

"What?"

"He always has been," she murmured sleepily. "Don't worry. I'm not in contact with him or anything. He just added me as a friend years ago when I first set my Facebook up."

I looked at my wife, but she was already falling asleep, her eyes closed, her face serene.

I picked up my phone and scrolled through Isla's friends

list. There were several guys with the first name Alex, but I knew which one it was because he did look similar to the man who'd served around the hot tub earlier.

"There you are," I said to myself because Isla's slow, deep breaths indicated that she was asleep. "The guy who used to make sex tapes with my wife. I wonder what you're up to these days."

I clicked on his profile, but it was private. I couldn't see anything more than his profile picture and basic information.

"Ah well," I sighed. It was time for me to sleep. And maybe dream about my gorgeous redhead wife and her ex-boyfriend.

What I didn't know then was that my dreams were about to come true.

———

The morning sun spilled generously through the vast windows of the spa, casting a warm, golden hue over the room where Isla and I were to have our massages. Lying on adjacent tables, the tranquillity of the spa wrapped around us like a cocoon, I found myself divided between closing my eyes to savour the masseur's skilled touch and stealing glances at Isla. She lay serene, a picture of relaxation, her red hair fanned out on the pillow, the gentle rise and fall of her back a rhythm I found more captivating than the ambient music softly playing in the background.

My masseur, a tall, silent type with hands that spoke more eloquently than words ever could, worked his way methodically, easing the tension from my muscles. Yet, it was the sight of another pair of hands, strong yet gentle, gliding over Isla's skin, that ensnared my attention. The way the masseur's fingers moved with such professional ease across her shoulders, down the curve of her back, and along the length of her legs stirred an unexpected feeling within me.

I wondered, with a hint of a thrill, whether he found the same pleasure in his work when his hands were on her as I would. Did he notice the softness of her skin, the graceful lines of her body, the way she subtly shifted under his touch? Did he imagine what her tits and pussy would look like, if she rolled over onto her back uncovered?

The session ended all too soon, yet the image lingered, fuelling a mix of emotions as we dressed and left the sanctuary of the massage room. The day passed in a comfortable blur, with leisurely walks through the spa's lush gardens and moments of quiet reflection by the poolside, our conversations meandering and light.

By evening, as we sat down to our last dinner in the spa's dimly lit restaurant, the previous night's confessions resurfaced. We were in a booth, a private bubble amidst the clinking of cutlery and the murmur of other diners and it was then, over plates of exquisitely prepared food, that Isla broached the subject of Alex once more.

"So," she started, her voice casual but with an undercurrent of curiosity, "After last night, did you get in touch with Alex on Facebook?" Her emerald eyes met mine across the table, gleaming with a mixture of mischief and genuine interest.

The question took me by surprise, not because I hadn't thought about it—because, in truth, I had, more than I cared to admit—but because of the openness with which she brought it up again. "I... well, I did look him up," I confessed, setting down my fork, unsure of how to navigate this conversation. "But his profile is private. Couldn't see much beyond the basics."

Isla leaned forward, resting her chin in her hand, her gaze never leaving mine. "So, you were tempted? Wondering if he still has any of those videos?" She was teasing but the question was still bold, flirting with stepping over a line, especially as we were in a public place.

"I'm not sure," I replied honestly, grappling with the reality of such an action. "It's one thing to fantasize, to talk about it between us. But reaching out, making it... real? That's different."

Her smile was understanding, yet there was a flicker of something else—anticipation, perhaps, or a challenge. "It is different," she agreed, her voice soft. "But isn't that the point? To explore something new, something a little daring?"

"You said he's deleted them," I reminded her.

"He did." Isla nodded, her face looking a little... what? Sad? Disappointed? Did she really want me to get in touch with him? The notion was insane. He'd think me weird or worse. "I made sure of it. Perhaps I should have kept copies. Just for myself, not for him."

The conversation lingered in the air as we finished our meal, a mixture of excitement and uncertainty accompanying each bite. The drive home was quiet. I was lost in my thoughts about the doors I might have opened by inquiring so much about Alex. The spa weekend had been a retreat, a pause from reality, but now, as we headed back to our lives, the fantasies we'd indulged in demanded consideration, blurring the lines between what was and what could be. And as the city lights came into view, marking the end of our journey, I realized that the adventure we were on was not just about exploring each other but about challenging the very boundaries we thought defined us.

———

Back at home, nestled in the familiarity of our own bed, the conversation we'd started in the dimly lit restaurant of the spa seemed to follow us, hanging around in the back of my mind. The city lights outside our window cast a soft glow, mirroring the flicker of unresolved curiosity that danced between us.

"So," I ventured, breaking the silence that had enveloped us since we'd turned off the lights, "Were you serious about wishing you'd kept copies of those videos with Alex?" My voice was cautious, threading carefully through my mix of desire and doubt.

Isla turned towards me, her silhouette outlined by the ambient light. "It was just a thought." Her voice was a blend of reflection and mischief. "And I had a sexy thought earlier, on the way home. I know he deleted those old videos... But imagine if I got in touch with him and suggested making a new one... A one-off sex tape, just for your eyes?"

My reaction was immediate, a mix of shock and intrigue. "Are you serious?" I asked, trying to decipher the earnestness in her tone.

She laughed. A quick, nervous sound. "Of course not, Ethan. I was just teasing you. Seeing how you'd react to such a... lewd suggestion." She was quick to retract, yet the flicker of genuine contemplation before her denial didn't escape me.

But the idea, once planted, grew roots in the silence that followed her laughter. "But what if," I found myself asking, the words leaving me before I could weigh their impact, "Hypothetically, of course... if I said 'yes', would you do it? Isn't that... wouldn't that be like cheating?"

Her body stilled beside me, and for a moment, I wondered if I'd pushed the boundaries of our fantasy too far. Then, softly, almost hesitantly, she spoke. "Hypothetically? I... I don't know. It's a fantasy, Ethan. Fantasies don't always align with reality."

"But in a fantasy," I pressed, my curiosity piqued by the seriousness of our hypothetical scenario, "If it was just about the excitement, the thrill for us... would it still feel like cheating to you?"

Isla was silent for a long time, so long that I thought perhaps I'd overstepped. Then, with a sigh that seemed to carry the weight of her thoughts, she answered. "In a fantasy, it's just that—a fantasy, it doesn't hurt anyone. But in reality, the lines are blurrier. If we both agreed, if it was something we both wanted, then... maybe it wouldn't be cheating."

Her words, careful yet open, sparked something inside me. A powerful, urgent curiosity and an overwhelming temptation to push this as far as I dared.

"Keeping this hypothetical... Would you be tempted to do it for yourself as much as you would for me? I know you'd love to give me the sex tape I've always wanted but wouldn't you be tempted just by the sex? By his big dick? You always say he was amazing in bed. Would you be tempted to experience that again, one more time?"

The room felt charged, the air between us thick with the unspoken. I watched her, trying to read the nuances of her expression in the dim light. Was that a flicker of desire in her eyes? Her hesitation spoke volumes.

"Maybe," she whispered, her voice betraying a vulnerability and excitement I'd seldom seen. "It's a horny thought. To be naughty like that again, to feel that... sluttiness."

The admission stirred something primal in me. The thought of Isla with him, making a dirty video for us, ignited a complex web of emotions. I reached for her, my movements deliberate, tracing the lines of her body with a newfound hunger. Our conversation had unlocked a door I wasn't sure we could close again—not that I wanted to.

As I touched her, my hands finding her breasts, her nipples stiff to my touch, the hypotheticals blurred into reality. She responded with an urgency that matched my own, her skin hot under my fingers. Our mouths found each other, and we kissed passionately, stripping each other from our nightwear.

"So, if I said 'yes'?" I found myself asking, my voice thick with desire as I slid my cock inside her, beginning to fuck her slowly. "Hypothetically, would you want to do it? For us but for yourself too?"

Her breathing hitched, and in the heat of the moment, she confessed, "Yes... hypothetically. I'd fuck him if you wanted me to." The word hung between us, a caveat, yet the truth in her voice was unmistakable.

I fucked her hard and she fucked me back, pushing her hips upwards to meet my every thrust, taking my cock as deep as she could, her legs wrapping around my back.

"I know he's single," she whispered while we fucked. "I saw on his feed a while ago that he's split from his wife. Divorced."

"So, he'd probably leap at the chance to hook up and fuck you again," I replied, pumping my cock in and out of her rapidly at the thought. Why did this turn me on so much?

It seemed to excite Isla just as much. She was moaning softly in my ear the whole time, in between teasing me with statements of how she wondered if his cock was still as big and hard as it used to be all those years ago.

"Perhaps you need to find out," I teased her back.

And then, in the climax of our union, after we'd both come and we were lying there, trying to get our breath back, she asked, her voice serious despite our fervour, "Were those questions really just hypothetical, or do you... do you want me to reach out to him?"

Her question made my heart skip a beat. I'd just come and yet I was still more turned on than I could ever remember being before. "The thought turns me on," I breathed against her skin. "I can't deny that. But only if it's what you want too."

She nodded, a silent agreement that sealed our pact. We were venturing into uncharted territory, guided by our mutual desire to explore the boundaries of our relationship. And as we lay there, spent and entwined, the reality of what we'd proposed hung over us like a promise. A promise to explore, to challenge, to dare.

And so, our fantasy, once whispered in the dark, became a

potential reality, a thrilling, terrifying prospect that promised to redefine us. The strangely arousing visions of this morning, of the masseur's hands gliding over my wife's body were nothing compared to the visions I had in my head now—of Alex fucking my wife.

———

The morning light felt different somehow as if the dawn of the new day carried with it the weight of our whispered promises from the night before. Isla and I got ready for work in comfortable silence, a stark contrast to the intensity of our conversation and actions just hours earlier. We exchanged the usual pleasantries, the kind that spouses share when the day ahead looms large and time is a thief. We didn't talk about Alex. In fact, it was as though the sexually charged conversation and the daring agreement we'd made hadn't happened at all.

As I drove to work, the rhythmic hum of the engine and the familiar route offered a semblance of normalcy. I found myself trying to shrug off the previous night as nothing more than heated talk fuelled by passion and desire, words amplified by arousal but not meant to be taken seriously. It was easy, in the light of day and amidst the demands of work, to relegate our exchange to just another fantasy.

Throughout the day, my mind wandered, drifting back to Isla's voice, her words, the serious tone that had threaded through her query as we'd fucked. But no, it was madness, wasn't it? The fantasies of the night had no place in the light of day.

That evening, as we sat down for our meal, the casual setting belied the tumultuous undercurrent of my thoughts. The day had passed without further mention of Alex, without any indication that we would revisit the subject. Perhaps Isla, too, had recognized the folly of our nocturnal musings.

Then, without preamble, Isla shattered the illusion of it all just being a fantasy—with four simple words.

"I contacted Alex today," she said, her voice steady, her emerald eyes meeting mine across the table. "We had a long chat, catching up."

The words landed with the force of a physical blow, shocking in their suddenness, their implications. For a moment, I was rendered speechless, the myriad of responses jumbling together in a tangled mess of shock, disbelief, and an undeniable surge of excitement. The conversation hadn't been just talk; it hadn't gotten out of hand. It was real, and Isla had taken the first step into making our whispered fantasy a tangible possibility.

I struggled to find my voice, to form a coherent response. "You... you did?" was all I managed, my mind racing to catch up with the implications of her revelation.

"Yes," Isla continued, her voice calm but carrying an undercurrent of something I couldn't quite identify. "We just talked about old times, about where life has taken us since... It was nice, catching up."

The simplicity of her statement did nothing to ease the turmoil inside me. Questions clamoured for attention, each demanding precedence over the others. Had the conversation veered into the territory of our fantasies? Had she mentioned the possibility of creating a new tape, of rekindling an old flame for the sake of a shared desire?

"Is that all?" I had to ask. "You just... caught up."

"He told me about his divorce," Isla nodded, continuing to eat and I did the same, trying to calm my heart which must have hit a hundred beats a minute. "He cheated on her and got caught. I have zero sympathy for him."

That information should have been a relief, a signal that Alex was not the ideal candidate for any kind of reconnection, let alone one of such an intimate nature. Yet, my heart still raced, not slowed by her words. The fact that she had reached out, that they had conversed, was a threshold crossed. But had it been merely a catch-up, or had they crossed into the territory we'd speculated about so fervently?

The silence that followed was heavy, loaded with unasked questions and unvoiced thoughts. Finally, I found the courage to ask, "Did... did you mention our conversation from last night?"

Isla paused, her fork midway to her mouth, and then she set it down, her gaze meeting mine squarely. "Yes, I did," she confessed, her voice steady but soft.

The admission felt like a punch to the gut. "What did he say?" I managed to ask, my voice tight with a mix of dread and anticipation.

She took a deep breath before answering. "I asked him if he'd kept any copies of the videos we made, first. He said no, that he really had deleted them, just like I asked him to, years ago." Her eyes didn't waver from mine, and I sensed she was carefully gauging my reaction.

"And then?" I prompted, my curiosity a living, breathing thing between us.

"Then... I told him about your fantasy," Isla said, her voice a whisper now. "That you wished you could have watched those tapes. About how we'd joked... hypothesized about making a new tape. Then he saved me asking the question. It was like he'd read my mind. He said that if I was ever interested in hooking up, just to make a sex tape for you, he'd be up for it."

The room spun. This was no longer a hypothetical discussion, a fantasy shared in the darkness of our bedroom. It was real, tangible, a possibility laid bare by Isla's admission.

"What did you say?" The words were out before I could stop them, my voice barely above a whisper, fraught with an emotion I couldn't name.

"I was surprised, obviously," she continued, her gaze

never leaving mine. "But I didn't say no. I said I'd think about it, that it was... a lot to consider."

A lot to consider. The understatement of the year. The floodgates of my emotions burst open—jealousy, excitement, fear, and an overwhelming sense of the unknown.

We finished our meal in a kind of stunned silence, each lost in our own whirlwind of thoughts and feelings. This conversation had moved us into uncharted waters, the reality of our fantasies suddenly within arm's reach. And as we cleared the dishes, the physical proximity between us felt charged with a new energy, a silent acknowledgment of the precipice we were inching towards.

The night stretched out before us, heavy with the weight of our revelations. Lying in bed later, the darkness seemed to press in around us, dense with unspoken questions and the echo of possibilities we had dared to voice. This was no longer just about a fantasy; it was about us, our desires, our limits, and how far we were willing to push them.

After we'd made love, our passion fuelled again by the tumultuous emotions of the evening, we lay entangled in the afterglow, the silence around us thick with unspoken thoughts. It was me who broke the silence, the question that had been burning within me since dinner finding its voice in the quiet of our bedroom. "What happens next, Isla? Do you... do you want to take Alex up on his offer?"

"I don't know." Isla shifted to look at me, her eyes reflecting a myriad of emotions. "Do you want me to?" she countered, her voice soft yet laden with the weight of the decision before us.

It was a dance of words, each of us probing the other, seeking reassurance, confirmation. The enormity of the step we were considering pressed in on me, a tide of anticipation and fear. Yet, beneath it all, there was an undeniable spark of excitement, a curiosity that refused to be quelled.

"Yes," I admitted, my voice a mere whisper, the word

feeling like a key turning in a lock. "Yes, I think I do. But only if you do, Isla. Only if it's something you want to do."

Her hand found mine in the darkness, her grip firm and reassuring. "I do," she said, her voice carrying a decisive edge. "I feel guilty for admitting to it but I want to. For us. For the thrill of it. Just once."

The mutual admission hung between us, a new understanding, a pact of sorts. Then, without another word, Isla reached for her phone on the bedside table, the screen's glow illuminating our faces in the dim room. My heart raced as I watched over her shoulder, her fingers hesitating for just a moment before she began to type a message to Alex.

"You're doing this now?" I asked and she nodded.

"Before I change my mind," she explained, her fingers urgently tapping away on the screen.

+Isla

Hi. You up?

Alex was still awake and replied immediately.

The conversation was brief and direct. There was an immediacy to their exchange, Isla proposing tomorrow night for their meeting, Alex agreeing without hesitation.

+Isla

About hooking up. My husband likes the idea. Let's do it.

Alex

Oh hell yeah. Tell him I'll make him the best sex tape he's ever seen

Isla

I will. Are you free tomorrow night?

The speed of it caught me off guard, the reality of the situation crystallizing with every passing second.

"Tomorrow? Why so soon?" I asked, my voice betraying a hint of my surprise.

Isla looked at me, her expression resolute. "If I give myself too much time to think, I might back out. I'll get nervous, overthink everything. This... this needs to be something we dive into, Ethan. If we're going to do this, it's best to just do it. Get it out of the way before either of us changes our mind."

The logic was sound, even if the hastiness of it sent a thrill of fear through me. It was happening, the line between fantasy and reality blurring before my very eyes.

+Isla

Text me your address and a time. You better not let me down.

Alex replied with his street and house number and told her to come any time after seven. He promised her a drink and something to eat but Isla replied that she really just wanted to meet up and have sex. She didn't want any time to get nervous and overthink it. Then she added that maybe one drink—maybe two—might be a good idea, to take the edge off because she'd be nervous. Alex told her not to be nervous. She knew him.

And with that, Isla set her phone down, turning to me with a look of determination mixed with vulnerability. There was no turning back now. The die was cast.

The night that followed was restless, the anticipation of the meeting with Alex casting a long shadow over us both as we tossed and turned, neither of us sleeping soundly. Yet, despite the unease, there was a thread of excitement, a sense of adventure that neither of us could deny. We were on the brink of something new, something daring, and the promise of that experience and the sex tape that might come with it was both terrifying and exhilarating.

———

As dawn crept through the curtains, marking the arrival of the day that would see our fantasy inch closer to reality, we held each other, a silent acknowledgment of the step we were about to take. This was the day that Isla was going to sleep with another man, outside of our marriage. It felt weird to consider that and I realised she'd been right to arrange it so hastily. Even just one day was too long to think about it too hard without beginning to doubt the wisdom of what we were doing.

Throughout the day, my mind was a battlefield of conflicting emotions. I was consumed by a nervous energy that made it nearly impossible to focus on any task at work. My phone became a lifeline, the only tangible connection to Isla as we ventured further into uncharted territory. Our text messages served as both reassurances and affirmations of our mutual decision.

+Ethan

Still feeling okay about tonight?'

Isla

Yes. Nervous, but okay. You?

Ethan

Same. Nervous. But I trust you. We're in this together, right?

Isla

Absolutely. Together. No matter what.

The back-and-forth continued, each message a small step in bolstering our resolve, reaffirming our commitment to each other and the adventure we were about to undertake.

As the workday finally ended, a part of me dreaded going home, knowing Isla would soon leave for her encounter with Alex. Yet another part of me needed to see her, to reassure myself that our connection remained unbroken.

I found Isla in our bedroom, the image of calm amidst the storm that raged inside me. She had chosen her attire with care. Her little black dress clung to her in all the right places, enhancing her slim but curvy figure, while the hint of black lace peeking out at her cleavage told me that she was wearing her sexiest, see-through bra and panty set. Her make-up was done to perfection, her emerald eyes enhanced by smoky eyeshadow, and her lips were painted a sultry red.

"Wow," was all I managed to say, my throat tight with a mix of emotions.

She smiled, a soft, tender thing that reached her eyes. "I wanted to wait for you. To show you." Her voice was gentle, her hands smoothing down the fabric of her dress nervously. Her long red hair was down, the fiery waves rolling over her bare shoulders.

The intimacy of the moment, the vulnerability we both felt, was overwhelming. Isla stepped closer, her arms winding around me in a loving embrace. "I'll keep you updated, so keep your phone with you," she whispered, her lips finding mine in a kiss that was both a goodbye and a promise.

The tenderness of her kiss, the love that flowed between us, offered a momentary solace from the storm of emotions within me. As we parted, a silent communication passed between us, a reassurance that no matter what happened tonight, it would not define us. We were stronger than the sum of our desires, our fantasies. This was something we both wanted. Something we needed.

Watching her leave, the click of the door echoing in the empty house, left me in a state of heightened anticipation and anxiety. The hours stretched out before me, each minute an eternity as I awaited her messages, her updates.

The house felt unusually quiet, the silence amplifying the tumult of my thoughts. I tried to distract myself, to no avail. My mind was with Isla, imagining her with Alex, the scenarios both thrilling and terrifying.

Had a couple of drinks, her first message read, the ping coming from my phone making me instantly erect, the anticipation of what it might say simply too much. *Going to the bedroom now.*

As the evening wore on, the wait became almost unbearable, a test of my resolve and our trust. Yet, through it all, there was an underlying current of excitement, heightened when the next update came through, an hour later.

+Isla

Fucked once. It was unreal. He wants to do it again before I leave.

I typed a reply, not quite knowing what to say. She'd done it. She'd fucked him. My beautiful wife had enjoyed another man. It felt surreal but also incredibly hot.

+Ethan

I love you.

That was all I could think to type and almost immediately I received her reply.

+Isla

I love you too. More than ever. Thank you for letting me do this. I'll be home soon.

I wanted to go to bed and jerk off. I was unbearably turned on, but I knew that if I did, I wouldn't be able to recover in time to enjoy her when she got back. I switched on the TV, poured myself a glass of whisky, and tried to await her return calmly.

As the minutes ticked by, transforming into what felt like an eternity, the tension within me built to an almost unbearable pitch. The glow from the television screen did little to distract me from my racing thoughts, and the whisky, while soothing, couldn't dull the sharp edge of my anticipation. Isla's messages had ignited a fire within me, a confluence of emotions that ranged from excitement to a deep, resonant love for her bravery and trust in us.

Finally, an hour or so later, the sound of the key turning in the lock snapped me out of my reverie, my heart leaping into my throat as the door swung open to reveal Isla, standing there. Her hair was messed up, her lipstick was smeared. Her black dress, so immaculate before she left, was creased but she was still a vision.

Without a word, she crossed the room and enveloped me in a kiss that burned with intensity, her passion and desire palpable. In that moment, nothing else existed but the two of us, our connection reignited by her return.

The heat between us flared, our bodies responding with a primal urgency. Hands roamed. My clothes began to fall away as I stripped them off, ready to fuck her right here in our living room.

"Where are your panties?" I said, my hand pulling up her dress to reveal that she had nothing on beneath.

"He wanted to keep them," she moaned, her lips crushing against mine as I pushed backward towards the couch but then, suddenly, Isla pulled back, her breath heavy, her eyes alight with a mixture of emotions.

"Ethan," she began, her voice thick with unspoken intensity, "We need to stop. I want to tell you what happened... it was incredible. Almost too good."

The words hung in the air, a confession that both thrilled and chilled me. The reality of her experience, the depth of it, was something I hadn't fully anticipated.

"Too good?" I questioned, curiosity burning inside me.

"Yes. We did everything. And," she continued, her gaze locked with mine, "I got it all on video, just like we talked about. For you."

The revelation sent a new wave of desire coursing through me, tempered by a flicker of uncertainty. To see her with another man, to witness their intimacy—was I ready for that? Yet the thought was also undeniably arousing, a fulfillment of the fantasy we had shared.

We sat on the couch, Isla nestling into me as she reached into her handbag for her phone. "I want you to see it," she said, her voice a whisper of seduction and vulnerability. "But only if you're sure. This... this changes things, Ethan. It makes them real."

My heart pounded as I took the phone from her, the video queued up and ready. To press play was to cross a threshold, to see my wife in a way I never had before. The room felt charged, the air thick with the weight of our decision.

"I'm sure," I managed to say, my voice steadier than I felt. "I love you, Isla. Nothing changes that."

And so, with a deep breath, I pressed play. The screen came to life, revealing Isla and Alex, sitting on the edge of his bed, the phone propped up nearby to catch whatever happened next.

"I sucked his cock first," she whispered, the words sending a shiver of anticipation through me.

The image of Alex—looking just like he did on his Facebook profile, tall and handsome and not as old as I'd expected him to look—stood up, stripping off his shirt and dropping his trousers and shorts to reveal an impressively long and very erect cock.

"You… You weren't lying when you said he was big," I said, struggling to find my voice.

"I wasn't lying about anything." We slipped into silence as the Isla on the screen stripped off her dress and removed her bra seductively for her ex-boyfriend, who was toying with his dick as he enjoyed the show.

Watching it, I felt a myriad of emotions—jealousy, arousal, love—all tangled together in a complex web.

Then she slid down her panties and knelt on the floor in front of him.

"I struggled to get him in my mouth again," she purred from beside me, both our sets of eyes trained on the screen.

My wife's mouth wrapped around the head of his cock, sucking the tip of it, making Alex moan softly, then she curled her fingers around his thick shaft and tried to take more, slowly moving down his length inch-by-inch.

"Oh my God," I heard myself whisper, scarcely able to believe what I was seeing. Isla worked more of his cock into her mouth, playing with his smooth, shaved balls while stroking the base of the shaft until eventually, the tall man put his hand in her hair and pulled her head savagely onto his length.

"I gagged again," Isla confessed as the image of her tensed on the screen, coughing around the thick cock that was suddenly rammed down her throat. "But I managed it."

I watched as Alex aggressively throat-fucked my wife and as the video played, Isla watched me, searching my face for any sign of regret or discomfort. But what she saw was acceptance, a deep-seated arousal that matched her own. The sight of her being used by this stranger was a turn-on like nothing I'd felt before and she saw it, smiling to herself.

Then Alex stopped her, bending to scoop her into his arms and tossing her easily onto the bed, pushing her thighs apart roughly and diving his head between them to enjoy her pussy.

I noticed she'd trimmed her fine red pubes into a tidy triangle, while shaving completely around her pussy lips, giving him free roam with his mouth, and within moments, Alex had Isla writhing on the bed in ecstasy, his tongue pleasuring her expertly.

"He's so good with his tongue," she murmured, her hand sliding over my thigh to feel the hard lump in my jeans. "I see you're enjoying it so far."

"I am," I said, my voice hoarse.

As the scene unfolded on the screen, a potent blend of emotions coursed through me. Witnessing Isla in such an intimate moment with someone else was unlike anything I had ever experienced. It challenged me, pushing me to the edge of my comfort zone and beyond, into a realm of raw emotion and primal desire.

Isla, sensing the tumult within me, reached for my hand, her touch a grounding force in the storm of my feelings. "I tried to remake every sex tape we'd ever done together," she said softly, her words an anchor in the swirling sea of my thoughts. Her voice brought me back, focusing my attention on her, on us, and the incredible journey we were on together. "I thought it would be fun for your sex tape to be a kind of 'best moments' compilation. A bit of everything."

As Alex positioned himself above Isla on the screen, her body quivering from the orgasm he'd just given her, a back-arching, toe-curling climax, I held my breath. This was it. His huge cock dangled there, the tip of it hovering above my wife's pussy.

The hunger and chemistry between them was undeniable —raw, unfiltered, and overwhelmingly real. It was a stark reminder of the risk I'd taken tonight. Would she even want me again after this?

Then he pushed it into her. There was no finesse. He placed the head of his big cock against my wife's moist, pink folds and then shoved it in, making her body tense and her voice to cry out loudly, the sound echoing in the bedroom on-screen and in the front room where we sat.

"I felt like he was splitting me in two," Isla said, releasing my hand and unbuttoning the front of my jeans to pull out my throbbing erection.

I didn't reply. I sat there, entranced as I watched Isla's ex take her in front of my eyes. There was no other word for it. He spread her legs, pinning her knees back - and then he just fucked her, bringing her to another climax after several minutes of rough, animalistic fucking.

"Did he come…" I couldn't finish the question but Lisa knew what I was going to ask.

"Inside me?" Her hand slowly stroked me as I watched him thrust into her one last time, the muscles in his back clenching. "Yes. He filled me up good."

The first video ended, and the screen went dark after he turned and collected his phone, but the intensity of the moment lingered in the air between us. Isla turned to me, her eyes searching mine for a reaction, for any hint of regret or discomfort. What she found instead was a profound love and an awe for her courage and trust.

"This changes nothing between us," she said, her voice steady with conviction. "If anything, it brings us closer. Tell me I'm right."

"You're right," I said, after a long moment of trying to absorb what I'd just seen.

Isla's response was a smile, a soft, knowing expression that spoke volumes. We had ventured into unexplored territory, faced our fears and desires head-on, and emerged stronger for it.

"There's another video," she reminded me, taking the phone to start the next sex tape and then handing me the phone back.

On this one, my wife was riding him. Alex was on his back while she straddled his cock, carefully mounting it and then sliding up and down his length, the camera handheld this time so she could record the penetration close-up.

It was so surreal, seeing the familiar sight of Isla's pussy lips—shaved smooth for her former lover—stretched out around a cock twice as thick as mine. She lifted herself up so that only the tip remained inside, then slowly lowered herself until she'd taken every inch, her body fully impaled on his long dick, her pussy pressing against his balls.

"Fuck," I moaned, unable to take it anymore. "This is fucking crazy."

"You like it, right?" Isla asked, lifting her dress, and climbing onto my lap. When I nodded, unable to pull my attention away from her bouncing up and down on her ex-boyfriend's cock, she took me inside her and I paused the video to acknowledge something.

"Oh, wow," I gasped at the sensation of her pussy. "I can tell you've been fucked."

"He left me gaping a little," she confessed. "He really

stretched me out. I've got some of his cum inside still. I hope you don't mind."

That was why her pussy felt cool and slick. I should have been grossed out, but I wasn't. When I looked down to see my cock smeared in a mixture of Isla's and Alex's juices, I didn't care. It was startlingly real now. Another man had cum inside my wife.

I pressed play on the video again as Isla slowly ground her pussy on my cock, her fingers finding her clit and toying with herself and I watched as she moved onto all fours after a while, Alex pounding her savagely from behind in that position for a while.

Then the video finally came to a close with my wife doing as she was instructed, dropping to her knees so that Alex could finish on her face.

"You said you liked the thought of him coming on my face and tits," she said, pushing down onto my cock, taking me fully inside her. "So, I let him."

I watched as he jerked his huge dick until several long spurts of white sperm shot from the tip, hitting my wife on the forehead and chin. She opened her mouth, sticking out her tongue and catching another spurt—which she swallowed eagerly—and then her ex-boyfriend jerked out more cum, this time aiming at—and hitting—Isla's curvy breasts.

"I loved him coming on me," she sighed, her fingers rubbing her clit urgently. "Marking me as his. It's such a fucking turn-on."

Then she climaxed, the feeling of her well-fucked, loose cunt tensing around my cock the final thing I needed to cum too. My cock pulsed inside her, my cum joining Alex's, dribbling out and pooling around the base of my shaft until eventually, the video ended and our sex with it, Isla slid from me, took my hand, and led me upstairs,

The rest of the night was a blur of emotion and connection, a reaffirmation of our love and commitment to each other. We talked, laughed, and held each other, basking in the afterglow of our shared experience. It was a pivotal moment in our relationship, one that deepened our understanding and appreciation for one another.

"I have to admit," my wife said, her fingers pushing hair out of my eyes to stare into mine with her beautiful emerald gaze, "Tonight was the best sex I've had in a long time. Not just the sex with Alex, but the sex with you. It was such an amazing turn-on, watching you—watching me—have sex with another man."

"I feel the same," I replied honestly. "I was worried at one point... worried that you might not feel the same about me, after being with Alex again. But then the sex we just had... I enjoyed it more than I've ever enjoyed anything."

"Me too," she giggled, the musical sound of her light voice breaking the intense seriousness of our conversation. "I can't believe I've been so naughty and slutty. I feel young again, like when we were first dating."

"I feel the same," I confessed, enjoying the sight of her gorgeous smile. "The nervousness, the anticipation, the build-up, waiting for you to come home. The buzz I feel now afterward. It's like nothing I've ever felt."

"I was nervous too. I know what you mean," Isla nodded, her red hair slipping into her face so that she had to push it back. "The sex with Alex was so fucking good, I won't lie, but on the way home, I was so turned on and yet scared about your reaction... It's like an adrenaline rush."

"It is," I agreed. She was right. "And now I have my very own sex tape of you and him."

"You do." Isla pushed herself up to a half-sitting position, gazing at me while resting on her elbows. "What would you say if I suggested that it's the first sex tape but not the last."

"What do you mean?" I replied, liking what she was suggesting. "You want to fuck Alex again, don't you?"

"Yeah," she nodded, her red hair tumbling over her shoulders. "Not just him."

"Then who else?" I said slowly. I hadn't expected this.

"Look who I have on my Facebook now," she teased me, passing me her phone again after bringing up a particular profile.

The young guy from the hotel gazed back at me.

"No way," I grinned.

"I can't go back in time and fuck young Alex for you, but he's the next best thing."

Then she leaned forward and kissed me. This was going to be fun.

Paul Garland is a celebrated British author of over fifty erotica books, covering themes ranging from cuckolding and hot past stories to teasing tales of size queens and adventurous hotwives. You can learn more about Paul and his books here:

https://www.amazon.com/author/paulgarland
https://www.paulgarland.net

A TASTE OF SOMETHING MORE

Lacey Cross

The sun warms my skin as Lawrence and I get out of the car, the picturesque vineyard stretching before us with rows of lush grapevines. The air is thick with the scent of earth and ripening fruit. We hear faint laughter coming from the path leading down to a charming rustic barn. The owners have converted it into an event space, which Lawrence's company has rented for a dinner party. It promises to be an enjoyable evening.

I brush my hands down my red sundress, smoothing the skirt. The light fabric clings to my breasts like a second skin before billowing out into a full skirt. The neckline dips dangerously low, hinting at the valley between my breasts. It's a dress designed to entice, to make men imagine peeling it off me or pushing it up.

"Fuck, baby, you're a vision," Lawrence murmurs appreciatively, his arm snaking around my waist to pull me flush against him. His lips graze my ear, sending pleasure racing down my spine. "I'll be fighting men off all day."

God, I hope so. We recently experimented with me fucking someone else and he let me choose whoever I wanted. I chose his boss, Heath, who will definitely be here today. Since that night, Lawrence and Heath have become better friends and occasionally meet up at the pub. I guess bonding over their shared love of my pussy has brought them closer. The thought of seeing Heath again sends a jolt of electricity through my entire body, making my core clench. I can hardly contain my excitement.

I turn in his embrace, my body molding to his, and I can't help teasing him. "Maybe I want you to fight them off... or maybe I want you to share me."

Lawrence's eyes darken, and his fingers dig into my waist. "Behave, you little minx. I'll share you when I'm good and ready."

My wonderful husband never explicitly stated it, but I can tell he's planning on fucking me when we get home... at least I hope so. If not, I'm going to have to use my wiles to seduce him. I don't want to go to bed without an orgasm tonight.

I slide my hand in Lawrence's, and we stroll towards the festivities. Coworkers cluster in small groups, chatting as they sip wine and nibble on gourmet appetizers. Even though Lawrence and I don't drink anymore, the laid-back, adults-only atmosphere is a pleasant change from the usual family-oriented company events. But beneath the surface, I'm buzzing with anticipation as I daydream of forbidden pleasures that include Heath's cock inside me tonight.

As Lawrence and I make our way through the crowd, a sense of power builds inside me. I'm here to be desired, to be lusted after. Ever since I fucked Heath, I feel like a sexual goddess. Becoming a hotwife has reawakened the sensual side of myself that had been buried by years of marriage and the comfort of being with one man. Having more than just my husband burning for me is a heady feeling, and whenever one of his coworkers' eyes linger on me for a second too long, a thrill runs through me.

But my thoughts soon turn back to Heath. What would it be like to have him pounding inside me again with that raw intensity that left me breathless? Jesus, am I going to be like this at every company event now that I've fucked his boss?

As we approach a group of coworkers, I glimpse Heath from the corner of my eye. My heart skips a beat, and I try to steady my nerves. I try to get involved with the conversation around me for a bit, but I'm too distracted by thoughts of fucking Heath.

I murmur to Lawrence that I need a drink, and he squeezes my hand before I wander off. I'm reaching for a cool glass of ice water when I feel it—the scorching weight of a hungry gaze raking over my body. My nipples tighten, straining against the thin fabric of my dress. I know who's eye-fucking me. It's Heath.

Slowly, I pivot to face him, my pulse thrumming in my ears. He's across the barn, looking yummy in fitted khakis and a blue button-down shirt stretching across his broad chest. The sleeves are rolled up, exposing tan forearms corded with muscle. I want to feel those arms pinning me down while he fucks me senseless.

Our eyes lock, electric heat arcing between us. The rest of the world fades away until there's only Heath, undressing me with his piercing blue gaze. I'm instantly transported back to that dark alley behind the pub on St. Patrick's Day, the bricks scraping my back as he pounded into me. I'd love to wrap my hands around that thick cock of his and hear him moan at my touch.

My core clenches again and I feel my panties growing wet. I squeeze my thighs together, desperate for friction, and take a long sip of water. Heath's eyes follow the movement, his lips curling into a knowing smirk.

Lawrence joins me, a low growl rumbling in his chest as he notices the mutual eye-fucking. "Easy, baby. We don't want to scandalize my coworkers."

I drag my gaze away from Heath, giving Lawrence my

flirtiest look through my lashes. "Maybe I want to scandalize them, so they see what a lucky man you are?"

Lawrence grins. "Oh, they know, sweetheart. They can smell how desperate you are for cock. I bet that pretty little pussy is dripping already, isn't it?"

"God, yes."

I love how he's embraced the dirty talk since the night I fucked Heath at the pub. It's opened up something in my husband, and it's fabulous.

He skims his hand up my back, fingers teasing the soft skin above the edge of my dress. "Filthy girl. Keep being a cock-hungry slut and I'll fuck you right here in front of everyone."

"Promise?" I moan softly as my clit throbs. I know he doesn't really mean it, but just the thought of him taking me while a group of people watches is the right kind of filthy to my brain.

"I don't think they could handle the heat," he teases as he gives me a quick kiss. "Now let's mingle. I want to show you off."

Reluctantly, I disentangle myself from Lawrence, and we drift towards a group of his coworkers. Would Lawrence even let me fuck Heath again now that they've become friends? Every time I glance Heath's way, he's watching me, still undressing me with his eyes. Desire simmers in my core, making me ache. This is torture, but I love it.

Lawrence spends the next thirty minutes brushing against me often. Every slight caress makes me shiver and imagine multiple men touching me. Yeah, my husband knows exactly what he's doing.

Eventually, I leave him discussing the merger of a rival company to check out the food. I'm so distracted, I don't notice Heath approach until he's right beside me at the table, his presence mesmerizing.

"Mia," he says, his deep voice vibrating through me. "You

look good enough to eat. I could skip the food and just devour you instead."

I suppress a moan at the thought of his mouth on me and give him a coy smile. "Hello Heath, it's always a pleasure to see you."

His gaze drags over me, lingering on my tits as his lips quirk. "Oh, I could really make it a pleasure. I've been thinking about that tight little pussy all night—about bending you over and sinking my cock into your slick heat just out of earshot of everyone."

My breasts heave as I inhale sharply, my pussy buzzing at the thought of his cock deep inside me. "Jesus." I hold in a moan as my knees go weak. "You can't just say things like that."

"Why not? It's true." He leans in closer, and I can smell his cologne, cedar and citrus. Intoxicating. "I know you're dripping for it. I could fuck that greedy pussy and make you beg to come."

We both know he could, based on what happened the night at the pub when he did just that. I'm dizzy from arousal as I think about all the naughty things I want him to do to me. My breasts ache and my panties are a mess. I want to climb him like a tree and ride his cock until I explode.

I whimper, "Heath, I can't. Not here."

"I think you can. I think you want to." His hand brushes my hip, a featherlight caress that sets me on fire. "There's a spot behind the barn, hidden from view. I could lift up that gorgeous dress, rip off those dripping panties, and fuck you. You'd come so hard, you'd have to stifle your screams to hide how much of a little slut you are."

"Oh god." My skin is feverish and I'm crazy turned on. It would be so easy to let him take me, fuck me, ruin me.

He reaches into his pocket to grab something and then presses it into my hand. I glance down, shocked when I see the tattered black lace panties he tore off me on St. Patrick's

Day. Holy fuck, he went back for them? All thoughts drain from me as I'm consumed with longing.

When I look at him, his blue eyes blaze into mine. "Meet me behind the barn in five minutes. Don't make me wait." It's not a request, but a command.

Then he's gone, striding away like he didn't just set my panties ablaze with his filthy words. I'm left reeling, my pussy desperate to be filled. Yep, I'm a slut all right.

Dazed, I look around for Lawrence. He's right where I left him, deep in conversation with another coworker. As if sensing my gaze, our eyes meet and when he looks past me, I realize he's watching Heath walk away. Lawrence raises an eyebrow, his expression dark and hungry. Slowly, deliberately, he nods.

He's giving me permission.

I'm going to let another man fuck me while my husband waits for his turn. The thought makes me dizzy with need.

I set my glass down, my panties still balled up in one hand, and slip away from the party. My heart pounds as I round the corner of the barn, the laughter and conversation from the party sounding faint through the barn walls. Heath is waiting, and he wastes no time pressing my back to the rough wood.

"I knew you couldn't resist me," he rasps, his hands already pushing up my dress, just as I hoped would happen. "Dirty girl, so eager for my cock."

"Please," I whine, beyond shame.

I've been daydreaming about his cock ever since the first night with him. But it's more than just his cock. I need him to make me feel like a filthy slut and fuck me hard.

He tears my panties off, the lace fluttering to the grass. "Beg for it."

Opening my fist, I let the black panties flutter to the ground to join the other pair. Maybe he will take them both home this time.

I'm too far gone to care how desperate I sound. "Please fuck me! I need your cock. I'll do anything."

"That's it, baby. Let me hear you." He pulls his cock out of his pants and lifts my leg to give him better access.

He teases my pussy with the tip of his cock, shallow thrusts designed to drive me mad with lust. It works.

I hold on to his shoulders and moan, "Please, I'll be your slut, your whore, anything. Just fuck me!"

With a savage growl, he slams into me, splitting me open on his thick cock. I bite off a scream as my pussy molds around him. He sets a brutal pace, pounding into me, the wet slap of skin on skin filthy and delicious.

"Fuck, you feel amazing," he groans. "So fucking tight. I'm going to ruin this pussy."

"Yes, ruin me," I sob as I cling to his shoulders.

He fucks me harder, grinding his pelvis against my clit with every thrust. I lose myself in the feeling of his cock pummeling me as the pleasure builds in layers.

Just when I feel like I can't take any more, he pulls out and turns me around, shoving my face against the wood. He knows exactly how rough to treat me. I lift the hem of my dress to my waist and spread my legs, offering myself up to him. I can feel the sticky trails of my juices coating my inner thighs as I wait for him to fuck me.

Within moments, he rams into me, my pussy devouring every inch. Spirals of bliss radiate from my core with every thrust as he picks up the same punishing rhythm. One hand tangles in my hair, yanking my head back, as the other grasps my hip with bruising force. My toes curl, and I can feel myself hurtling towards the edge, my orgasm building with each delicious thrust.

When he reaches around to toy with my clit, I detonate. The bliss overwhelms me, and stars burst along the corners of my vision as waves of pleasure wash over me. Slapping my hand over my mouth, I muffle my cries as he fucks me through my orgasm. A part of me wants people to hear what a dirty slut I am… that I'm fucking my husband's boss just on the other side of the barn wall. I want the entire world to know just how filthy I am.

When I stop shaking, Heath pulls out and makes me face him, pushing me to my knees. The ground is dusty and knowing I'm going to look a mess when he's done with me gives me an illicit thrill. He aims his cock at my mouth, and I open wide, taking him without hesitation. I swallow his thick length all the way to the base. He moans, tugging on my hair as he fucks my mouth, using me like the filthy little slut that I am. I can smell and taste myself on him and it makes my head reel. This is beyond anything I imagined would happen, and I love it.

I look up, our gazes meeting, as I hollow my cheeks and suck harder. I'm determined to give him as much pleasure as he just gave me.

He groans, "Such a good cocksucker," and I hum happily around his shaft as I continue to lick and suck for all I'm worth. My hand slides between my legs, fingering my pussy, matching his thrusts.

Within moments, another orgasm hits and I writhe as the pleasure surges through me. I suck on him furiously as my climax reaches its peak. He lets out a strangled moan and pulls his cock out of my mouth right before he comes. What's he doing? I wanted to taste him!

He yanks me up by my arms and shoves me against the wall. There's a wildness to him that makes me quiver with need as he pulls my leg up to his waist. He supports me while he pins me to the wall and slides his cock into me.

"Ooooh, god!" I cry out as he stretches me once more, the pleasure almost too much to take.

He hammers into me, gripping my ass with an almost painful intensity as he huffs, "Did you think I wasn't going to fill you full of cum? You're going to have my seed dripping out of you for the rest of the night."

Oh fuck, I will, because he destroyed my panties. As we surge together, I claw at his shirt, mewling out little peeps and moans as he drives into me with determination. Wrapping my other leg around him, I surrender myself to the wildness of the moment.

When his thrusts become quick and shallow, I can tell he's about to lose it. Thinking about how dirty it's going to be standing around while his cum runs out of me almost tips me over the edge again.

"Come for me, slut," he commands in a dominating tone. "Let me feel that pussy squeeze me. Milk my fucking cock."

He kisses me to muffle my cries. Our tongues wrestle as my toes curl from the exquisite pleasure. I detonate with a silent scream, my pussy spasming wildly around him as ecstasy ripples from my fingers to my toes. Through my fog of desire, I feel him swell inside me, his cock jerking as he fills me full of hot, sticky cum. It seems like it goes on forever as the pleasure peaks and then recedes.

My head is spinning when he finally stops fucking me, and I slump in his arms, boneless, my dress bunched around my waist. He continues to hold me up, his softening cock still buried in my fluttering pussy. I feel deliciously used.

"Jesus, that was intense," he pants. "You're incredible."

I nuzzle into him, drunk on endorphins. "Mmm, you're not so bad yourself."

He chuckles as he carefully sets me back on my feet. After putting his cock back into his pants, he helps me straighten my dress. I'm a mess, my hair wild and my thighs sticky with our combined wetness.

"What happens now?" I ask, suddenly uncertain. Am I supposed to go back to the party and hope no one notices how wrecked I am?

Heath tucks a strand of hair behind my ear, his touch

surprisingly gentle. "Now, you go back to your husband. And later, when you're lying in bed, I want you to remember this. Remember how good I fucked this sweet pussy."

God, he really knows how to say exactly what I need to hear to make me feel like a filthy slut.

"I will," I vow breathlessly.

With a final searing kiss, he turns and strolls back towards the party, leaving me weak-kneed and trembling.

I take a moment to collect myself and attempt to straighten my dress and brush my hair with my fingers. Oh god, I need to visit the restroom before I go back to the party. There's no way I don't look freshly fucked.

The bathroom mirror tells me all I need to know. My cheeks are flushed, my hair is exactly as messy as I thought it would be… I'm debauched. It's wonderful.

I quickly make myself look presentable the best I can. It's time to find my husband. When I step into the barn, Lawrence's eyes burn into mine as I approach. He takes my hand and squeezes it.

"Have fun?" he asks, his voice strained with longing.

"Mmm, so much fun." I wind my arms around his neck, playing with the short hairs at his nape. "But I'm not done yet. I need my husband's cock."

Lawrence's eyes flash, his grasp on my hips tightening as he croons, "My dirty, insatiable slut. I'm going to fuck you so hard it erases any trace of him."

"Yes, please." I capture his lips in a kiss before pulling back. "Remind me who I belong to."

I almost giggle when he makes a loud comment about showing me the vineyard, as if someone is going to care that we leave the barn together. Hand in hand, we slip away from the party. I'm giddy, drunk on pleasure and anticipation.

We make it as far as a tiny outbuilding with some wooden crates next to it. He lifts me and sets me on the edge of a crate, and I eagerly spread my legs for him as he fumbles with his pants. When he pulls out his cock and pushes my dress up, I see the moment he realizes I'm not wearing panties anymore.

He pauses, his expression hungry, and I love it. Then he swears, his eyes dark with desire. "Someone's panties seem to be missing."

I can't resist teasing him. "That's because someone's boss ripped them off of me the same way he did when we fucked on St. Patrick's Day."

"Fuck, You're such a dirty girl."

My lack of panties sends him into a frenzy, and I lean back, gripping the edges of the crate while he slams home in one swift thrust. This time when I cry out, I don't cover my mouth. I don't care if the entire world knows I'm fucking my husband.

He jackhammers into me so hard my breasts bounce. His cock hits a wonderful spot deep inside me and I almost have an out-of-body experience. It's like I'm hovering above us, watching him fuck me, and I moan in an increasing crescendo the closer I get to another orgasm.

I don't know how many times I've come today—is this three, or is it four—but this one is massive when it hits. I buck against him, chanting, "Fuck me, fuck me... fuck me!" repeatedly as waves of pleasure radiate outward. My eyes roll back in my head and all I can feel is the bliss rippling along every nerve ending in my body.

Just as my body starts to go slack, he stills and holds himself buried as deep in me as he can. He grunts and I feel his cock twitching and pulsing, unleashing a torrent of hot, creamy cum. He slowly thrusts his cum back into me and I imagine his seed mixing with Heath's.

Holy fuck, that was so dirty. I feel absolutely destroyed, both physically and mentally. If he asked me what my name was right now, I'm not sure I could tell him.

When he pulls his cock out, he wraps his arms around me,

holding me and rocking me while I shiver from the intense pleasure.

"Are you okay?" His voice is husky and full of love. The obvious concern for me is adorable after thoroughly ravishing me.

I murmur, "Mmm hmm," and rest in his embrace, enjoying the floaty feeling.

When I can think a little more clearly, I look up at him. The sex haze clears slowly from Lawrence's eyes, but the heat doesn't dissipate. He smiles and says, "Fuck, I love you. You're such an amazing little slut."

I moan a little, feeling that delicious tingle that only the perfect word can elicit from me. "Mmm, I think you're the amazing one. That was incredible. I like you having control over who I fuck and when."

His eyes are stormy with lust. "Oh, I think you'll see how much control I'll have soon. Now that I've shared you with Heath, I feel like I owe it to myself to make you into a bigger slut."

God, that sounds good to me. My pussy flutters at that statement and I tip my head up, silently begging for a kiss. He brushes his lips against mine before helping me off the crate.

I grin, squeezing Lawrence's hand. "I love you. Thank you for letting me be me."

He lifts our joined hands, pressing a kiss to my knuckles. "I love every part of you, baby. The good girl and the cock-hungry slut. Never hide from me."

"Never," I vow, my heart swelling with love and gratitude.

Now I understand why all our friends are trying out the hotwife lifestyle. This is fucking fabulous, and I can't wait for our next adventure.

. . .

This story isn't the first with Mia, Lawrence, and Heath. If you want to read Mia's first hotwife experience when she fucks Heath against the wall of the pub, check out March Hotwife at: https://www.lacey-cross.net/hotwifemia

Lacey Cross is a wife sharing erotica writer with over 100 short stories published since she started in 2021. Her stories emphasize the pleasure found from the wife living her best slut life. She explores themes of freeuse, submissive hotwives with dominant bulls, BDSM... and oh-so-many men.

A TALE OF TWO SIXTIES

Delores Swallows

I t was the best of times, it was the worst of times. Gary squeezed his eyes shut as he pumped his cock. *It was the age of wisdom, it was the age of foolishness.* The image of his wife in her late twenties filled his mind's eye. She smiled down at him as she rode him. Her sex was slick and hot having just come, and now it was his turn.

She licked her lips and bounced harder. "Haven't you got something for me?"

"Oh yeah."

"So what are you waiting for? Give it to me."

Gary pumped his hand faster, pushed the quilt down to his thighs, and ejaculated over his stomach. He let out a muted groan, then pumped again to drain the rest of his frustration from his blue balls. The vision of a twenty-eight-year-old Anita clenching her inner muscles and welcoming his seed faded. He reached over for tissues and wiped the mess from his body.

He and Anita had been together for almost forty years, married for thirty-seven of them. They'd met when they were both hired by the same pharma company shortly after they'd graduated. Anita had been in a relationship with a guy from university called Simon. He'd got a job in a different part of the country, and Gary was persistent.

They had gone out for a couple of innocent 'drink after work' dates, and after a trip to the cinema to see the newly released *Beverly Hills Cop*, they'd shared their first kiss. The next time they went out for a drink, the date lasted until it was time to get up for work the following morning. Just a few months later, they'd moved into a rented flat together, and the following year bought their first house and got married.

Their careers progressed and they made the most of their holidays, taking trips to Australia, Indonesia, South America, and India. Most of Gary's fantasies came from memories from those times: the two of them groping each other under a blanket on an evening boat trip through Sydney harbour. Anita wearing an oversized t-shirt with nothing beneath it as they found a secluded part of the beach in Bali. A five-minute knee-trembler against a sheer rock face on the Inca trail.

And now, all these years later, he was reduced to jacking off alone while his wife caught up with the latest episode of *Bake Off* downstairs in their living room. He couldn't pinpoint when things had changed. It had been a gradual erosion. They'd had two kids in the nineties, bringing them even more happiness, and those kids had now grown into wonderful adults with spouses of their own.

He and Anita were still a happy, loving couple, though the burning passion they'd once shared had undoubtedly been extinguished. Lying in their bed, heart rate still elevated from his orgasm, he decided it was high time the two of them talked about it. They were sixty, not dead.

———

It wasn't until early Sunday evening, three days after Gary had decided to raise the issue, that a suitable opportunity arose. They'd both spent time in the garden, him cutting the back lawn while she dead-headed the roses. Having showered, they lounged on recliners on the patio, each sipping a well-earned G&T.

"Guess what I was thinking about the other night?" he asked, trying to keep his voice casual.

She turned to him, her big blue eyes settling on his face. "What?"

"Bali."

"Ah..." She smiled. "We always said we'd go back there one day."

It wasn't the tropical island he wanted to return to. "I was remembering the night we lay beneath the stars outside our beach hut."

"Hmm."

He could tell from her embarrassed smile that she remembered it, too. "I miss those times," he said, "and I'm not talking about the places we visited."

Anita's smile disappeared, and she let out a sigh.

"Don't you miss that sort of closeness?" he persisted.

"Are you saying you no longer feel close?"

"No." He squeezed her hand. "You're the centre of my world and always will be. It's just..."

"Just what?"

He shrugged, already regretting starting the conversation. "I miss the intimacy we shared. The sex."

"It's not like we never—"

"Can you remember the last time we made love?"

She paused, obviously struggling to answer. "It was... I'm sure it's not that long ago."

"And I'm sure it is."

"God, Gary, it's not like we're still twenty-five."

"No, but we still have a pulse, and we both still have needs."

This made her blink. "What are you saying?"

"I'm saying I'm back to behaving like a teenager, jacking

off to stop me from going stir-crazy."

Anita stared, eyes wide. "And you think I need to know that?"

Another wave of regret washed over him but he shrugged it off. "What do you want me to say? I still get urges, and I still get horny."

"I'm sorry. It's just that I'm often tired after work."

"If you're tired, you could come to bed earlier."

"And I'm no longer the firm, fit young thing I once was."

"You've never lost your figure—"

"I'm heavier than I was back then, and breastfeeding ruined my boobs."

He laughed and shook his head. "That's not true. I know how good you look naked, and I can't believe you don't see it too. You're in much better shape than a lot of women twenty years younger."

"Oh, so you're looking at younger women are you?"

"That's not what I said."

She drained her glass and stood up. "I'll go and start dinner."

After she'd gone back inside, Gary let out a long sigh and wondered why he'd bothered.

They ate in relative silence, talking about their upcoming weeks at work. Although they'd originally both worked in Research, Anita had moved to the Regulatory Department after a few years. Gary then left the company and got a job working for a bank, managing a small group that maintained the IT network. It involved occasional travel to other branches and regular trips to the London headquarters. Gary would be going down to London later that week.

After dinner they watched TV and then, as usual, Gary went to bed shortly after ten. Anita had always been a night owl and often stayed up until after midnight during the week, and even later when she didn't have to get up for work the following day.

Gary was reading a novel when Anita came into the bedroom. He glanced at the clock; it was only ten-forty. Anita visited the bathroom and came back smelling of toothpaste. She slipped into bed beside him, then browsed on her phone for a while.

"So," she said eventually, her eyes still on the screen of her phone. "Have you had a wank tonight?"

He laughed, closed his book and put it down. "No, but thanks for asking."

She looked at him, her face serious. "Do you do it a lot?"

"No."

"How often?"

"Just when the urge gets…" He shrugged. "You must do something to relieve yourself, too."

She blinked, obviously caught off guard. Then she frowned. "No, I—"

He smiled. "Don't deny it. I've been honest with you."

Still frowning, she shrugged. "Sometimes I might…"

"Rub one off?"

She laughed and slapped his arm. "Don't make it sound so dirty."

"I'm not making it sound dirty. It's nothing to be ashamed of." He narrowed his eyes. "So, where do you do it?"

"I'm not—"

"Come on, I told you."

She let out an exasperated sigh. "It depends. Sometimes in the bath, or lying in bed when you've already got up." She smiled. "I did it in the living room one night watching 80's music videos."

That was a lot of times. The thought of Anita making herself come all over the house thrilled him more than he cared to admit, but it was a double-edged sword. If she was horny that often, why hadn't she instigated sex with him? Did it mean she no longer found him physically attractive?

"Where do you come?" she asked.

"Sorry?"

"Us girls can do it without causing too much mess, but it's different for men. I haven't noticed stiff little stains on the sheets, so what do you do?"

"I use tissues."

She nodded, watching him with a hint of a smile. It was weird the way admitting that they still masturbated seemed to have lowered the barrier that had built up between them.

"So," he said, pushing his leg against hers. "Can I watch you make yourself come?"

"No chance."

"What if I really want to watch you?"

"Why don't you just fuck me instead?"

It was an offer he would have jumped at earlier. "No, I like the eroticism of watching you touch yourself."

"Eroticism?" She sounded incredulous.

Gary nodded. "I find the idea of you masturbating really sexy, and I'd love to see you do it."

"But I'm offering you *real* sex. Penetration, copulation, and the exchange of body fluids."

They had only had sex a handful of times in the previous year, and it'd been over four months since the last one. Gary knew if he went inside her now, he'd finish far too quickly.

"I've already told you what I want."

She sighed, then pushed the quilt down to their knees. "You do it first, then."

"That wasn't the deal."

"We never had a deal, and I think it's only fair that you go first."

"I could go second."

Anita shook her head.

Gary was now faced with a conundrum. In the ideal scenario, Anita would bring herself off, then he could go inside her. As she'd have come already, it wouldn't matter how brief their sex was. But he also realised that if he didn't agree to her terms, she might well refuse and he'd end up getting nothing.

He didn't have a choice. "Okay."

She gave a grin and lay on her side facing him, elbow dug into the pillow, head propped up on her hand.

Gary reached down and stroked his cock through his boxers. It had thickened during their conversation but it was a long way from hard. "I'm not used to an audience. I might get stage fright."

"I'm sure you'll be fine."

He took a breath and decided to enjoy it as much as he could. After less than a minute's stroking through the soft cotton, he was fully hard. He raised his bum and eased his boxers down to his thighs, then started to pump his hand with a slow, twisting motion.

"Want me to get you some tissues to come into?"

He shook his head. "I'll come on my stomach, then clean it off with tissues."

"Oh, good." She smiled. "That'll make a better spectacle."

Gary closed his eyes and increased the speed of his strokes.

"Don't you use baby oil?" Anita asked.

He opened his eyes and shook his head.

"When I was seeing Simon, he liked me to jerk him off with oily hands."

This was something they'd never discussed before, but he found it appealing. "How often did you do that?"

"God, I can't remember." She shrugged. "Half a dozen, maybe."

"And did you let him watch you bring yourself off?"

She smiled and shook her head. "No, you'll be the first person to witness that."

Gary's relief lasted only until she added, "He liked to make me come with a courgette or cucumber."

He was discovering all sorts of secrets. "I can go raid the fridge later if you like."

She laughed, then turned serious. "Now stop talking and let me see you come."

Holding her gaze, he got back to the matter at hand, as it were. He wanked himself faster, and his breathing became shallow. Anita moved her focus down to his dick. He gave three hard pumps and stilled his hand. His cock twitched as a thick jet of cum arced up and landed on his chest.

Anita gasped, and Gary resumed his wanking motion. A second rope shot out, reaching almost as high as the first, then two more that landed on his stomach. Now breathless, he held his cock still and squeezed the base. The dying embers of his orgasm oozed from the crown, dribbled down his shaft and over his fingers.

When Anita looked back into his face, her eyes were wide. She placed her hand on his cum-splattered chest and rubbed it into his skin, matting the chest hairs in the process, but he didn't care. Her hand moved lower, smearing the cum over his stomach, then lower still. He released his cock and she wrapped her fingers around it. She held the shaft and repeatedly ran her thumb over the wet, sensitive tip.

Leaning close, she kissed him gently on the lips. "Thank you for letting me watch that."

Gary waited, not wanting to spoil the moment but dreading her turning over and going to sleep.

She left him hanging for a few seconds, then raised her eyebrows. "I suppose you're expecting to watch me now?"

He held his breath and nodded once.

She rolled onto her back and ran her hand down her body until she reached her crotch, then stroked herself through her panties for a little while. Just as her breathing changed, she raised her hips, ditched her panties, then lay back with parted legs to resume stroking her fingers through her folds.

Gary could smell her musk and see the juices coating her

fingers as she cupped her hand over her mons. Anita closed her eyes and rocked her wrist. Leaning forward to get a better view, he saw her second and third fingers dipping into her channel with each downward push of her wrist. She rocked her hand faster, the fingers going inside to the second knuckle. He could hear squelching and quiet moans. Eventually, she pulled her hand back and splayed her slippery fingers.

Massaging both sides of her clit, Anita sucked in gasps of air through gritted teeth. Suddenly, she opened her eyes, looked directly at Gary, parted her lips, and let out a grunt. Then she pushed her fingers back inside and jerked her body, riding her hand while moaning and sobbing. Her thighs trembled, her ragged breathing stopped for a moment, then she let out a long exhale and removed her hand.

Gary stared at her in awe. It was the sexiest thing he'd seen in a long time, and he wished he was young enough to go again. His mind was more than willing, but he just couldn't manage two erections in ten minutes. He'd have struggled to manage that in his thirties.

Anita opened her eyes, a delightful hint of embarrassment in her expression.

He ran a hand down her thigh, which was still trembling. "Fuck, you're sexy."

She laughed and shook her head. "I can't believe I let you watch that."

"I'm so glad you did. What were you fantasising about?"

She shrugged. "Oh, the usual. Some tall, dark, and handsome guy who sweeps me off my feet, takes me to his room, and rogers me senseless all night long."

Gary felt his jaw drop. Every time he jacked off, he fantasised about his wife – admittedly a younger version, but it was always about her.

"Sorry, should I have pretended I was fantasising about

you?" She had a mischievous glint in her eye, which made him laugh.

"No. The next time I do it, I'll probably fantasise about you giving oily hand-jobs to your old boyfriend while he pleasures you with produce from the vegetable rack."

Anita squealed and slapped his arm, laughing.

He held her hands. "Thank you for letting me watch. Right, I need to get cleaned up."

Standing beneath the hot jets of the shower moments later, Gary's mind kept going back to how fabulous Anita had looked mid-orgasm. The fact she'd been imagining getting fucked by another man gave him a dirty thrill he couldn't explain. And as for her jacking off her ex while he pleasured her with a make-do sex toy...

He returned to the bedroom to find Anita sitting up in bed.

She looked at him as he slid in beside her. "I'm sorry if you've been feeling neglected lately."

"The last half-hour almost made up for it."

She hid her face. "I still can't believe I let you see that."

"It was sexy as fuck, but I got other good stuff, too."

She looked puzzled. "What stuff?"

"Now I can think about you giving your ex oily hand-jobs."

"You can't possibly like that idea."

"Why not?"

"I just assumed... I never told you because I thought you'd be jealous."

"Nope. The thought of it actually turns me on. It added to the eroticism of our evening." He almost stopped there, then decided to say the rest. "And so did the idea of you fantasising about being swept off your feet and rogered silly by another man."

Anita blinked, her expression suddenly serious. "You don't mean that."

"I actually do. The thought of it is…" He sighed. "More so now I've seen you in the throes of ecstasy without being involved myself."

"You'd want to *watch*?"

Gary hesitated, partly because he was ashamed to admit it but also because he didn't want to make her angry.

She smiled. "Having second thoughts, are we? Backing down?"

"Any second thoughts are only because I don't want you to be hurt if I admit it turns me on."

"You find the idea of me with another man a turn-on?"

His pulse raged in his ears. "Would you hate me if I said yes?"

"No." She chewed her lower lip. "I'm shocked, but I certainly wouldn't hate you."

"See, that's brought even more eroticism to our evening."

"Hmm." She raised her eyebrows. "Will you fantasise about that for your next wank?"

"Why let it remain just a fantasy?"

"Don't tempt me!"

Their eyes locked and butterflies took flight in his stomach. She held his gaze for about ten seconds, then raised her eyebrows as if daring him.

He had to swallow the lump in his throat before he could speak. "Could you be tempted?"

"Like you said, I still have a pulse."

"Wow!"

"Wasn't that the answer you expected to hear?" There was a playfulness in her smile.

"To be honest, it wasn't a question I ever expected to ask."

"And now that you have?"

"Now, I think the eroticism has just shot up through the roof."

"You like the idea?"

Gary swallowed again, then nodded. "Probably more than I should."

"I don't think there's anything wrong with you liking the idea, but that would be kind of… selfish of me."

"Why?"

"Because I'd be the one getting the most out of it."

"I don't know about that," he said. "I expect the other guy may find it mildly pleasant."

"Bastard!" She turned serious. "I was referring to you. I'd be getting more out of it than you would."

"I don't think that's entirely true."

"What would you get out of it?"

"I got a huge thrill out of watching you play with yourself."

"Watching me masturbate is a lot different to watching me have sex with another man."

"Yeah, I guess so." His entire body seemed to thrum with anticipation. "But then again, having me watch you come on your fingers is a lot different than having me watch you come on another guy's cock. Maybe it'd be too much for you, too."

Anita stared at him in silence for several seconds. "I think I could cope."

He smiled at her answer.

She kept her expression serious. "Could you?"

Could I? "I guess there's only one way to find out."

Anita took a deep, shuddering breath. Her cheeks were slightly pink, and he saw how much it excited her. He knew there'd be no going back on his decision, so he started to think of a way to get into a situation where it might happen. Maybe they could book a room in a city hotel and try to find a suitable guest. Whenever Gary visited the London headquarters, he was always one of several lone guys in the hotel bar during the evenings.

"When are you in London this week?" she asked.

Evidently, she was thinking along the same lines. "I go Thursday, come back Friday."

She nodded. "Okay, I'll arrange it for Friday night, then."

"*What?*"

"If we leave it any longer, you'll get cold feet." She shrugged. "Or I will."

"But Friday won't give us much time to find another—"

"I'll get Liam."

Gary's mind raced. "Liam from your office?" She'd worked with the guy for years. His wife had died in her forties.

"He's moved departments, but we still meet up for lunch every so often."

Is it just lunch?

"While I know my fantasy is about a stranger," she continued, "I think I'd prefer it to be someone I trust. You know, a friend."

Gary nodded as if he understood her logic, but a voice in his head whispered that maybe she and Liam were already lovers. "Is Liam seeing anyone at the moment?"

"I don't think so." She smiled. "And I know he finds me attractive."

"How do you know that? Does he make a pass every time you meet for lunch?"

"Of course not. He's always the perfect gentleman, but I catch him looking at me sometimes. Checking me out."

"And how will you broach the subject of the two of you having sex while I watch?"

"I don't know, but I have a few days to work out a strategy."

Gary pondered in silence.

She pressed her leg against his. "What are you thinking?"

"I'm horny."

She laughed and shook her head. "You'll have to wait until after Friday."

"What? Why?"

"It'll give you something to look forward to." She raised her eyebrows. "Doesn't that add to the eroticism, too?"

———

During the week, Gary found it impossible to focus and was dreading his visit to head office because they always had issues he needed to concentrate on. Anita refused to divulge if she'd mentioned Friday to Liam, so by the time he left for London on Thursday morning, he was in a state of near panic. He had to work late on Thursday evening, so by the time he got back to his hotel and phoned Anita, it was nine-thirty.

"Hi," she said, sounding a lot more at ease than he felt. "How's your day gone?"

"Hectic but okay. I should be able to leave in time to catch the early train and be home for six."

"That sounds perfect." She paused, forcing him to ask the question.

"Perfect because...?"

"Liam will be arriving at seven-thirty."

"You've arranged it?"

"Mm hmm." When he didn't reply, she added, "Isn't that what you wanted?"

He closed his eyes and tried to control his breathing. *Is it what I want?*

"Gary?"

"I'm here. Yeah, I'm still up for it. I just didn't know if you'd be able to arrange it, that's all."

"You think I'm too old to pull a man?" Her voice was light and teasing.

"It's not that. I'm sure you'd have no shortage of willing men, it's just..." He sighed. "I can't begin to imagine how you raised the subject."

"Well, us women can be tactful, diplomatic, and persuasive."

"Which of those three skills did you use the least?"

She giggled down the phone. "He didn't take much persuading."

A hundred questions ran around in his head, but he couldn't bring himself to ask any of them.

"Gary, I need you to tell me it's what you want, and that there'll be no recriminations afterwards."

"There won't be."

"So, say it."

"I just have. There'll be no rec—"

"Not that bit." She sighed as if exasperated. "You have to say what you want to happen."

"Okay, I want to watch you with another man."

"Say it!"

He sighed. "I want to see you *get fucked* by another man."

"Thank you. I just needed to hear you say it, so I know it's still what you want. You've had a few days to think about it."

"I've thought of little else. Someone asked my opinion in a meeting on Tuesday, and I hadn't a clue what they'd been discussing."

She laughed. "What did you say?"

"Well, us men might not be tactful or diplomatic, but we can bullshit."

"Typical. So, getting back to tomorrow night. You're going to watch me get fucked, and after Liam has left, you get your turn. Right?"

"Right."

"Well, I suppose I should let you get some sleep. I need to have a bath and shave my legs."

"Just your legs?"

"Yes, you pervert. Right, I'll see you tomorrow."

"Night, love." He ended the call and dropped his phone onto the bed.

After using the bathroom, he undressed and got into bed. His mind immediately went to what would take place tomorrow evening, and he soon had a full erection. He gave it a tentative stroke, determined to save himself. His resolve crumbled because he knew he'd get no sleep otherwise. As he slowly pumped his cock, it struck him as ironic that only last week he was fantasising about fucking his wife when she was in her twenties. Now, he was fantasising about someone else fucking her at sixty.

———

Gary had a fitful night's sleep, then struggled through another five hours of not being able to concentrate on network-related issues before making his way to Euston and catching the train home. Since any attempt to read during the journey would be a waste of time, he gazed out of the window and considered his predicament as the countryside whizzed by unnoticed.

A vague, niggling thought that had been lurking in the background all week suddenly came into focus. Was this all a ruse? Would he arrive home to find Anita wearing a smile and little else, admitting she'd never intended asking Liam, or anyone for that matter?

And if that proved to be the case, would he be relieved or disappointed?

He still didn't know the answer when the taxi dropped him off at home just after six. The house looked freshly cleaned, and there was a smell of cooking coming from the kitchen. Anita was nowhere to be seen, so he headed upstairs.

"Hi," she called from their ensuite. "Can you use the other bathroom for a shower?"

"Yeah, no problem."

Ten minutes later, he emerged to find their bedroom and bathroom empty. He could hear Anita sorting crockery in the kitchen, so he dressed in casual trousers and a shirt, then went downstairs.

In the kitchen doorway, he stopped in his tracks. His wife looked stunning.

Anita smiled at his reaction. "You like?" she asked, turning a slow circle so he could admire her outfit. She wore a pale blue blouse and a long, dark blue wraparound skirt. Both seemed to be made of some silky material, and he was pretty sure he'd seen neither garment before.

The shoes, which appeared to consist of little more than two leather straps running diagonally across the instep and a two-inch stiletto heel, were definitely new. She'd painted her toenails the same dark blue as her skirt, and he was shocked to see her fingernails similarly adorned. He couldn't remember the last time she'd worn nail varnish. Her straight blonde hair was cut into a bob, and she counterbalanced the few grey hairs that had started showing by having dark lowlights added by the hairdresser.

"You look amazing."

"Thank you." She walked over and kissed his cheek, her perfume overwhelming his senses.

"How are you feeling?" he asked.

She chewed her lower lip, and he realised her lipstick was a darker shade than she usually wore. "I'm tingling all over."

He nodded. "Me too. Is yours a good tingle or a bad tingle?"

Before she could answer, the doorbell rang. Anita raised her eyebrows and a knot developed in his stomach. When she went to the front door, he headed through to the living room and remained standing until the others joined him. He stepped forward and shook Liam's hand. They exchanged pleasantries, which felt bizarre considering why the guy was there. They'd met on a number of occasions, but this time Gary studied him more closely. Liam was a little under six foot and in good shape. His short dark hair was greying at the temples, but he looked good considering he was in his late fifties.

Gary took the drink orders and poured them in the kitchen. When he returned, Liam and Anita were sitting together on the couch, so he took one of the armchairs. The three of them chatted a little about their roles at work, retirement plans, and what it was like working for managers who were twenty years younger than them. When Anita crossed her legs, her wraparound skirt fell open. Gary noticed Liam's eyes glance down before she pulled the material over her legs.

Anita had prepared nibbles, which they ate while talking about holiday destinations before Gary went to fix a second round of drinks. As he settled back into his armchair, he thought the other two seemed to be sitting a little closer together than they had been earlier. Anita re-crossed her legs, and this time she didn't bother to cover her exposed skin. Both men's eyes seemed to be drawn to her thighs, and as the conversation continued, the shoe on her hanging leg dangled off her foot. Gary thought it looked very sexy, and from the way Liam kept running his eyes in that direction, he was clearly of the same opinion.

"Gary asked if you were seeing anyone," Anita said.

Liam smiled and shook his head. "No, not for a while." He shrugged. "I suppose I'm stuck in my ways, and the thought of meeting women on a dating app fills me with dread."

"See, babe? He's single."

Gary felt his jaw drop, and tried to disguise his shock by pretending he was about to take a sip of his wine.

"So," Anita continued. "That means whatever happens tonight won't upset anyone."

Gary nodded mutely, looking from Liam to his wife.

She wasn't finished. "It won't upset you, will it Gary?"

He held her gaze for a second before turning his eyes on Liam and shaking his head. "No."

Anita smiled. "And it certainly won't upset me. So, I guess the only remaining question is..." She turned her blue eyes on Liam. "Will it upset you?"

Liam smiled and shook his head. "Not one bit."

"Perfect." She looked over at Gary. "I think we should have another drink."

Gary went to replenish their glasses. He returned to find Anita had closed the blinds and turned on a couple of lamps, giving the room an intimate glow. He settled back into the armchair and noticed Anita was now leaning against Liam.

"The other day," she said, smiling at Liam, "I confessed that I used to give my ex-boyfriend hand-jobs with lots of baby oil." She glanced at Gary. "I thought he'd be jealous, but he liked the idea."

Liam smiled and nodded at Gary. "I'm with you. I like the idea, too."

"Although," Gary said, turning the tables, "I didn't like it as much as the idea of your ex using a variety of vegetables to get you off."

"It's true." She leaned in so her nose was almost touching Liam's. "The bumps on a corn on the cob can feel really nice."

"I could check the fridge," Gary said, his cock already thickening from the way Anita was behaving.

"Why would I need that when I've got Liam?"

The men glanced at each other.

She leaned in harder, pushing her body against his. "I have got you, haven't I, Liam?"

He looked over at Gary, then back at Anita. "If that's what you both want."

"It's what we want. Right, Gary?"

"Yeah."

"See?" She leaned in and brushed her lips against Liam's. "He wants it. I want it." She kissed him gently again. "And I think you want it, too. Right?"

Liam kept his eyes on Anita's and nodded.

"Good." She pressed in and kissed him deeply, working her jaw and no doubt giving him her tongue.

Gary watched as his wife made out with another man, his mind bubbling with a potent cocktail of several cardinal sins. Pride and envy were definitely in the mix, maybe even a trace of greed, but the strongest flavour undoubtedly came from lust.

Anita dropped both feet to the floor and twisted to face Liam. His hand cradled the back of her head as their kissing got even more passionate. She ran her hands over his shoulders, the blue-painted fingernails scratching at his shirt. Liam traced a finger over her boob through her blouse, and Anita let out a low moan. This seemed to spur him on. He began caressing her full breasts, running his thumbs over the nipples.

In response, she made short work of the buttons on his shirt, pushed the two sides apart, and kissed his chest for a few moments before raising her head to kiss him again. Their breathing became ragged. She pulled back and helped Liam undo the buttons of her blouse. As Liam slipped his hands inside, Gary caught a glimpse of dark nipples showing through a white lacy bra that was also new.

Liam kissed her breasts through the lace as Anita lay against the back of the couch and cradled his head, moaning softly. After only a short time she eased his head away, reached between her boobs, and unclipped the fastener. As soon as she pulled the cups back, Liam advanced again, feasting on her tits, sucking noisily on the nipples. Anita let out urgent sobs, her fingers ruffling his hair as she pulled his head against her soft flesh.

Liam placed his hand on her bare thigh and her legs fell open as if he'd pressed a switch.

Gary held his breath as Liam slid his hand higher, face pressed to her chest, mouth still sucking noisily on a nipple. He saw a flash of white lace, then heard his wife's moans grow louder as Liam ran the tip of his finger over the gusset.

If watching her masturbate had been hot, seeing her with Liam was volcanic. But the angst of witnessing another man do these things to the woman he loved, and to see her reaction to it, was a bitter pill. While the thrill he got was through the roof, the gnawing pain of jealousy was undoubtedly there, eating away at him. But it didn't prevent his cock from swelling in the confines of his trousers, nor did it staunch the steady flow of precum oozing from his cock and soaking his shorts.

"Oh, fuck!"

His wife's voice brought his eyes back to between her legs, where Liam had slipped two fingers beyond the gusset. They were now buried as far as he could get them in her cunt, and Anita was rocking her hips on them. Liam's arm was pumping like a piston, his mouth now clamped on her other nipple. The smell of her juices was rich in the air, and Anita was taking short breaths through her mouth.

Suddenly, she opened her eyes and looked at Gary. He froze under her gaze, unable to do anything but stare straight back at her. Her breath caught in her throat, then she let out a grunt and bucked her hips faster as she came on Liam's fingers.

After a while she pushed his hand away and clawed at the buttons of his jeans, slipping her hand inside as soon as she could manage. She pumped her hand a few times before she withdrew it, shucked her panties, and lay back on the couch. One of her shoes had already fallen off. "Get your cock out."

Liam managed to push his jeans down to his knees before Anita pulled him down on top of her, scrabbling with one hand for his cock.

"Put it in," she hissed. "Put it in and fuck me."

As Anita rested one foot on the back of the couch and the other on the floor, Liam placed his knee on the cushion between her thighs and positioned his cock at her entrance. Gary's heart thumped in his chest as he watched another man's cock disappear between his wife's slick, engorged folds until the full length was buried.

"Oh yeah." Anita undulated on the couch and placed both her hands on Liam's buttocks, pulling him deeper. "Oh, fucking yeah."

Liam held his upper body up as he fucked her slowly. From the armchair, Gary had a perfect view. He could see Anita's face, her eyes fixed on Liam's, and her mouth open. He could see the entire front of her body, her boobs swaying in time to Liam's thrusts. And he could see Liam's cock, thick and glistening with juices as it slid in and out of her sex.

Gary wondered briefly if her choice of clothing was so she wouldn't have to expose her entire nakedness to Liam. The button-up blouse, wraparound skirt, and front-fastening bra allowed him full access to her body without the need to take anything off. Perhaps she was self-conscious, though Gary knew she had no reason to be.

"Oh, keep doing that." Anita rolled her hips and stared up into Liam's face. She hadn't looked in Gary's direction once since coming while being fingered. "Does that feel good?" she asked.

Liam nodded. Either he was too breathless to speak, or too polite to confirm her cunt felt good in front of her husband.

Anita licked her lips and shook a strand of hair from her face, then let out a breathy sigh. "Oh fuck. Fuck. Oh..." She raised her hips off the couch and cried out. Legs trembling, Anita bucked and twisted as another orgasm swept through her.

Liam increased the intensity of his thrusts. Anita clung to his back and rode him from below, her body coming up to meet his with a slap on each thrust.

"Come," she said, looking up into his face. "Come for me."

Liam squeezed his eyes shut, held his breath, and let out a long exhale. Anita pulled him lower and deeper, writhing beneath him, whispering encouragement as he flooded her pussy.

"That's it," she cooed. "Let me have it all." Finally, she turned her eyes to Gary.

He experienced an overwhelming sense of pride. She was his wife. Another man was filling her with cum, but she was *his* wife.

The couple on the couch eventually stilled. Liam pulled out and tucked his cock inside his jeans. Anita reached down for her panties and pulled them on. Gary sat forward a little to hide his erection.

Anita refastened her bra, then sat back and reached over to hold Liam's hand. "Thank you."

Liam laughed and shook his head. "I think I should be the one saying that."

She smiled, then looked over at Gary. "Is there any wine left?"

Gary nodded and walked out while holding his hand over the bulge in his trousers. He brought in a fresh bottle and poured a glass for Anita.

Liam held his hand up. "I probably shouldn't drink any more. I'm driving."

Anita groaned. "Oh, I assumed you'd stay the night."

What?

"I'll need to get back for Rufus."

Anita sighed. "Your dog will be fine. Besides, I've made up the spare bed..." She smiled at her husband. "For Gary."

Gary tried to keep his expression neutral. This wasn't something they'd discussed, and it certainly wasn't something he'd have agreed to.

"Well, I suppose I could have another drink." Liam held out his empty glass, which Gary filled with a trembling hand.

Had he been hoodwinked? In his mind, the evening had

been ideal up to now. Liam had fulfilled his role perfectly. He'd been good company during the drinks and nibbles, then passionate and respectful during the sex. Gary had enjoyed watching, and he knew Anita had enjoyed participating even more.

When she'd said Gary would get his turn after Liam had left, he'd never considered the possibility that Liam would stay the night. He felt like his balls were about to explode, and now he'd have to listen from the spare bedroom while Anita and Liam had sex again.

"So," Anita said, sitting back and snuggling into Liam while looking at Gary. "Was that as sexy as imagining me giving oily hand-jobs?"

"It was much sexier."

Liam wore a serious expression. "I have to confess, I thought Anita was winding me up when she suggested tonight."

Gary nodded. "If someone had told me a couple of weeks ago that I'd be sitting in this chair while she had sex with another man on the couch, I'd have thought it a wind-up, too."

Anita raised her glass. "Well, I'd like to thank you both. Here's to good times and sharing with friends."

The men both raised their glasses, then drank. An awkward silence ensued. While Anita and Liam were smiling at each other, Gary tried to decide if his wife's toast should be interpreted as tonight having been a success, or whether she was hinting that tonight was only the start.

The lack of conversation seemed to motivate Anita to move the evening to the second stage. She looked at Liam. "Should we take our drinks upstairs?"

He didn't even glance at Gary. "Okay."

Anita stood up and looked at her husband. "Will you turn things off down here?"

"Yeah, no problem."

"Thank you." She stepped over, bent, and kissed him on the cheek. "Don't worry, we're not cutting you out. I'll leave the door open and a light on."

Before he could answer, his now-barefoot wife led her lover towards the stairs. Liam was going to fuck her again, this time in the marital bed. Gary downed his drink in one, then hastily turned off all the downstairs lights before following them.

The door to the spare bedroom was diagonally opposite the master bedroom. Gary extinguished the landing light and walked quietly to the spare room. Leaving the room in darkness, he could see most of the king-sized bed where he usually slept. Tonight Liam was in it, lying on his back and staring up at Anita. She stood at the foot of the bed, her back to Gary as she faced the man who'd just fucked her. The man who was about to fuck her again.

She was talking quietly as she undressed. Gary couldn't hear what she was saying, but his earlier theory about her self-consciousness proved to be wrong. Evidently, she had no qualms about letting Liam see her naked as she seductively removed her blouse, skirt, bra, and finally her panties. Then she stepped to her side of the bed and slipped beneath the sheet. Gary held his breath and strained to hear their muted conversation. He could only make out odd words, his name was mentioned once, as was the phrase 'it was his idea'.

Had it been my idea? Gary couldn't actually remember, even though the conversation had been just a few days ago. He remembered admitting being turned on by her fantasies about having sex with a stranger, but the who-said-what details were fuzzy.

Anita pushed the sheet down and straddled Liam's legs. Then she bent over and started talking to him again. Although Gary couldn't actually see what she was doing with her hand, he was fairly sure she was playing with Liam's cock. When she lowered her head and Liam moaned, he knew exactly what she was doing. His wife was sucking the other man's cock.

Gary couldn't remember the last time she'd sucked his. It'd been at least fifteen years, maybe twenty, and he couldn't decide how he felt about her sucking Liam. Anita's head was now moving up and down at a steady rhythm. Liam had his hand resting on her head as he let out appreciative murmurs.

In the darkness of the spare room, Gary stood a few feet inside the doorway and squeezed his erection through his trousers. Another battle of emotions took place in his head. While part of him resented the fact she was treating Liam to something she'd denied him for decades, another part of him soared with pride. How would he react if Liam cried out and Anita gulped and swallowed? There was no denying the thrill Gary had got from watching another man flood her cunt. Would seeing him come in her mouth be even better?

He never got the chance to find out. Anita raised her head, crawled further up Liam's body, and impaled herself on his cock. Liam's hands roamed over her body, caressing her boobs, waist, and buttocks as she rode him. She dropped her head back, allowing Gary a view of her face, eyes closed and mouth open. After letting out a loud groan, she leaned forward and bounced harder on Liam as she reached her third orgasm of the evening.

Liam gripped her hips and yanked her back and forth on his cock, then rolled her onto her side and pounded her. From Gary's position, all he could see of his wife was one leg flung over Liam's thigh, but he could hear her moans. Liam's buttocks clenched and released, and Anita cried "Yes, yes, yes," as she welcomed his second load.

Gary stood stock-still. His cock was rigid inside his trousers, and his cum felt like it was trying to kick its own way out of his balls. Anita settled down beside Liam and pulled the sheet over them. She lifted her head and peered into the spare room, then reached over and turned out the light.

In the darkness, Gary quietly undressed and slipped into bed. His erection throbbed, but he was determined not to give himself the relief he craved. He lay awake for a long time, more than an hour, his brain running over everything he'd seen during the evening. The fact she'd bought new clothes for the evening had made it even sexier. She'd looked so good with her sexy shoes and painted nails, the long skirt pulled back to expose her legs, the front-fastening bra hanging open with her boobs on show. And she'd looked even better with Liam's cock buried bollocks deep inside her as she screamed her release and welcomed his.

Sleep finally came, but he was woken later by his wife's voice. He sat up and peered into the master bedroom, but this time Anita hadn't turned the light on. All Gary could do was listen to her quiet sighs and murmurs as Liam fucked her for a third time. Anita's moans grew louder, reaching a crescendo with her orgasm. Then she let out short gasps as Liam increased the force and speed of his thrusts chasing his own release. Although Gary never heard the other man make a sound, Anita's sighs and groans pinpointed when Liam had come. The house settled into silence again.

Gary was roused from sleep a second time when he felt the sheet being pulled back and the mattress dipping. Through the curtains, it looked like dawn was breaking.

"Good morning," Anita whispered, kissing his cheek, and snuggling close.

Gary looked towards the door.

"He's gone. He didn't want to get home to a kitchen full of dog pee, so he left five minutes ago."

"Ah."

"Shall we talk about it now, or are you going to fuck me first?"

His heart thumped in his chest. "I thought you might be

too sore." He wished it was light enough for him to see her face.

"I'm not too sore, but I suspect it's quite messy in there."

He rolled her onto her back and climbed on top. "Would you rather wait?"

She slid her legs open. "No. Would you?"

"No."

He pushed his throbbing cock into the molten core of her well-used cunt. They both sighed, though Gary's was probably louder. As he moved slowly in and out, Liam's cum seeped down her bum crack and soaked Gary's balls. The very idea of it gave him a thrill he couldn't put into words.

"I'm not going to last long," he whispered.

"I don't expect you to." She kissed his neck. "And I don't want you to. I just want you to add your mess to his."

Anita held him tight and squeezed down. Gary gasped and erupted, draining all the pent-up frustration of the last few hours, weeks, months, and possibly years. It was the most intense and satisfying orgasm he could remember. His entire body trembled, then a sated tiredness crept into every muscle.

"Did you enjoy the evening?" she eventually asked.

Gary wanted to see her face during this conversation, so he reached over and turned on the lamp. Anita blinked in the sudden light, then smiled. Her makeup was smudged, and her hair tousled. It was a sexy look.

He leaned close and kissed her forehead. "I enjoyed the evening immensely, though I got the impression that you enjoyed it even more."

"Wasn't I supposed to enjoy myself?"

"Of course you were. I wanted you to have a good time. From the sounds you were making all night long, I think it was mission accomplished."

She smiled and nodded, then frowned. "Weren't you even a little bit jealous?"

"I was incredibly jealous." Her eyes opened wide but before she could say anything, he added, "But my jealousy was outweighed by my arousal."

She smiled. "Good."

"And my pride."

"Pride?"

He nodded. "I was so proud of how good you looked and how you reacted to his touch. There were a whole host of emotions running through me as I watched the two of you on the couch. But also…"

"What?"

"I wondered if last night was the first time the two of you had ever—"

"It was." She sat up, her expression serious. "I promise. Nobody but you has ever touched me since we first started dating."

He smiled. "I'm sorry for asking, but—"

"It's okay. I guess it's only natural for you to have doubts after what I did."

Gary took a breath. "Can I ask you something else?"

She nodded.

"Do you see last night as a one-off experience, or the start of a new way of life?"

She laughed and shook her head. "Well, I certainly don't envisage making my way through a long line of suitors…"

He suspected she had more to say, so he waited. She chewed her lower lip, and he raised his eyebrows to show he wanted her to tell him what was on her mind.

"But I wouldn't mind repeating what we did last night."

"With Liam?"

She paused for a couple of seconds, then nodded. "I know I can count on his discretion."

"And now you know what his cock feels like."

She smiled. "Yes."

"And tastes like."

She frowned. "Did you see that part?"

"Mm hmm."

"Were you angry?"

He shook his head. "I couldn't decide if I wanted him to come in your mouth or not."

She sighed. "If we do repeat last night, I'd like you to join us."

"Join you, as in—?"

"I've never had a threesome, but I've thought about it many times over the years. I love the idea of being pleasured by two men."

Butterflies took flight again in Gary's stomach. "Is that what you want?"

She smiled. "I may be old, but I still have a pulse."

He laughed and pulled her into his chest. "Okay."

After reaching over to turn out the lamp, he lay back on the pillow and held his wife. Considering she'd spent the whole of last night having sex with another man, this was the closest he'd felt to her in years.

Delores Swallows has many dirty thoughts, and during his free time he writes them down in the form of stories. Born and bred in the northwest of England, he has a commoner's accent and a bit of a crush on his future queen. His stories often feature petite brunettes, high-heeled shoes and voyeurism. He claims he didn't realise these were obsessions until someone pointed out how often they appear in his work. Find out more about Delores on his website, chat on email or X.

AN OLD FRIEND (WITH BENEFITS)

Kenny Wright

"**A**m I the best wife or what?" Alexis said as we pulled the fresh sheet over the guest bed.

Glancing over at my wife, I openly checked her out. She was dressed for the gym, the heather gray leggings and racer-back top stretching tight over her trim, athletic body. That top did a particularly nice job showcasing her tits as she leaned forward to pull the bedsheet, her shoulder-length blonde hair falling forward, her bangs cutting across her rich, blue eyes.

"Yeah, definitely one of the best," I said, my eyes lingering in her deep cleavage.

Alexis laughed, raking her hair away from her face as she straightened up. She knew that she was attractive. She noticed all the attention she got just as much as I did but always downplayed it.

"Go on, I'll bite," I said. "Why do *you* think you're the best?"

She grabbed a pillow and stuffed it into a fresh pillowcase like it had wronged her. "Well, let's see. The kids are off to camp for two glorious weeks. We have the house completely to ourselves for the first time since *last* summer, when they went off. And I have let you invite your ex-girlfriend to stay with us for what should have been some sweet, hot, sexy time."

This wasn't the first time we'd discussed this, and while I knew that Alexis wasn't really mad, she brought it up enough that I knew she was at least mildly annoyed.

"First of all, Jaime isn't an ex—"

"Just a girl you had a lot of sex with—"

"Like twenty years ago! In college. We're better friends than…"

"Friends with benefits." She tossed the pillow on the bed and fluffed it. "In my book, she counts as an ex, and I should be jealous."

I rounded the bed and took Alexis into my arms. "You're not really jealous, right? You know that I've only got eyes for you, baby."

Alexis giggled. "I know *that's* a lie, but no, I'm not jealous." She wiggled free of me to finish making the bed. I couldn't help staring at her ass, which looked amazing in those leggings. "But you're still forcing me to be a host when I should be able to sit around in my sweats and do nothing."

"You can still do that—"

"And think of all the sex that you're going to miss out on."

"I don't think Jaime would mind." I pursued her, running my hand over that juicy ass.

Alexis shot me a look. "If you suggest that she join us, then I hope you like sleeping on the sofa, because this bed's taken."

"Never," I said. Although I'd definitely thought about that fantasy. I knew from experience that Jaime, my not-an-ex, was down for a threesome. "Just that we don't need to be embarrassed at being heard, like when the kids are in the house."

We finished with the duvet, tugging the corners into place to make a tidy bed. Alexis grabbed the old linens and tossed them into the basket. I made sure that the lamps worked. "I'm sorry, Alexis. I really didn't think about the overlap."

"I mean, it was on the family calendar."

"A calen... dar? What's that?"

Alexis tossed a towel from the basket at me and laughed. "It's the thing that you put your golfing weekends into."

"Oh, oh right. I thought that was just for golf."

"*Anyway...*" She turned on her heel and looked over her shoulder. "You owe me one for being such an amazing wife."

She caught me looking at her ass again. "Yes."

"I'm going to go take a shower; and when I'm out, you're going to spend our only afternoon alone between my legs, 'kay?"

I switched off the lamp. "You don't have to ask me twice."

———

"Oh!" Alexis always sounded surprised in those first moments when I go down on her. She giggled, inhaled sharply, and started cooing. "That's... that's nice, Peter. Uhnnn..."

It was definitely nice. I needed to do this more often. Alexis only got more and more beautiful with each passing year. She'd always been pretty, but now, at forty and after two kids, she was a true MILF. I loved her wider hips. I loved her fuller breasts, I loved how she took care of herself. Her beauty seemed so effortless, yet I knew how hard she worked for it. It was hot as hell.

I pushed a finger into her gash as I lapped up over her clit. Her spicy excitement mixed with the aroma of her body wash. She'd touched up her shave job, and her mound was deliciously bare and smooth.

I loved eating her out. We used to do this all the time. It had once been part of the deal for her to keep her pussy bare like this, but time and life and kids had gotten in the way of that. Oral sex was less a part of the routine, but the grooming stuck. As I listened to her gasp and moan above me, I resolved to do this more.

I pressed the tips of my fingers against her g-spot as I worked her clit. Her toes curled. She lifted one foot over my shoulder, a heel pressing into my neck. That's how I knew I was doing a good job. That and her cries.

"Haaa… uhhnn!"

I worked her to the very edge before backing off, letting her squirm, letting her beg. "More!"

"I'm a pretty great husband, too," I said, grinning up at her.

Alexis glared down at me, need and frustration all over her pretty face. "Fine. Whatever. Just don't stop."

I grinned, moving down to finish her when the doorbell rang.

"Ignore it," Alexis hissed. "Probably someone here trying to sell us new windows."

I started to get back to work on her when the doorbell rang again. This time, a bunch of times. Alexis groaned in frustration, flopping her head against the pillow.

"I'll get it." I rose. "I'm still dressed."

After splashing water on my face, I headed downstairs to see what this was all about.

"Jaime! This is a surprise."

On the other side of the door, her manicured finger about to press the doorbell a few dozen more times, was my friend, Jaime.

To use an old-school analogy, Alexis was the *Playboy* to Jaime's *Penthouse*. Both blondes were hot, they just presented it differently. It was hard not to compare—Jaime's hair was a lighter shade of blonde, longer, she was more petite, she had a small stud in her left nostril.

The differences went way beyond physical, though. "I know I was supposed to get in later, but I was able to work out a quicker route."

Case in point. Alexis, like most people, would have been considerate enough to tell the hosts that she'd be in early. Also, I had no idea if 'able to work out' meant something sexual, or more conventional, a question I just wouldn't have with my wife. Jaime had been fun as a fuck buddy in my twenties, but could get exhausting as a friend in our forties.

"Did you break your phone?" I asked.

"Hmm? No?" Then she got it. "Oh! Yeah, sorry I didn't text. It all got a little…" She shivered. "Intense."

Again, probably referencing the flights and running through airports, but maybe also fucking some airline attendant in the bathroom.

Jaime held her arms out wide. "How's it going, Peter?"

She didn't wait for a response. She pulled me in for a tight embrace that I could only return with a laugh.

"You two need a room?" Alexis asked from somewhere behind me. She wasn't being catty I heard the smile in the question.

"If you're offering," Jaime said, finally releasing me. "I do miss this guy's big dick sometimes."

Alexis laughed, looking right at me. "Remind me why I should be okay with letting her stay here?"

"Because you're a good person," I said.

"And because I'm fun," Jaime added.

Alexis had changed into a pair of tight jeans and a t-shirt —standard Alexis attire. She'd gathered her hair, still slightly damp, back into a messy bun, completing the girl-next-door look. "And mostly because I'm the best wife."

―――――

"Wait. Time-out. What's going on here?" I asked, feeling hot under the collar.

"We're just swapping stories from your past." Alexis batted her lashes at me innocently.

"Oh yeah," Jaime went on as if she hadn't heard me. "Your husband was a real man-slut."

"I prefer 'man-whore'," I corrected.

"Nah, you never did any of it for money," Jaime said. "And I'm also not sure why we always qualify men who do this, yet when a woman does it, we're just called 'slut' or 'whore,' like it's a given that women behave like that."

"Touche," Alexis said. "But more about my man-slut husband, please. You didn't, like, get jealous about that?"

Jaime actually laughed. "Jealous? No. We weren't exactly exclusive. Like, ever."

Alexis looked at me like she was looking at a complete stranger. At least she wasn't completely disgusted. I'd told her a few stories but had definitely understated things. Like I told her I only had six girlfriends, which was technically true, and more in line with her three boyfriends. What I left out was that I'd slept with over twenty–they just were never my girlfriend. Jaime was one of them.

I did tell her that my wildest experience was a foursome with Jaime, which seemed to intrigue Alexis when I'd made the confession, but she never pressed for details, and I didn't offer. Alexis's wildest experience was having public sex in the bathroom of a club, something I found hot as hell and always wanted to know more about but didn't dare ask. That could lead to more questions about my own past, and at the time, I was falling madly in love with Alexis and didn't want to fuck anything up.

It was different now, years later, but old habits die hard.

"But it wasn't so much him playing with other chicks that I remember—"

"Jaime," I warned.

"I think he got more pleasure watching me with other dudes."

"No," Alexis said, her hand over her mouth.

Jaime looked at me. "You never told her?"

"Told me what?"

"One of our favorite things to do was to go out to a frat party or bar, all dolled up—me, not him—and for Peter here to watch guys hit on me. Sometimes we left together and fucked each other silly. Sometimes, if he was hot enough, I'd hook up with a guy, and then go find Peter and tell him all about it."

Now Alexis was really looking at me like she didn't know me. Only she did. "You?" she asked.

"It was just a silly game." My face was on fire.

"It was so fucking hot," Jaime said right over me. "Don't get me wrong. Peter's not some cuck. He's a real man. You know that. He wasn't into humiliation or any bullshit like that. I think that's what made it so fucking... hot," she repeated.

"I just liked watching her get totally taken." I recovered some of my footing, thanks to Jaime's defense.

Alexis sat back, fingering the empty dinner plate in front of her as she turned this revelation over and over.

"Sometimes, he didn't even need to be there. Sometimes, I'd just text him that I met some hot guy out at a party. I'd ask if I should fuck him. Peter never said no."

"Wow." To me, Alexis said, "How come you never told me about this?"

"I didn't want to freak you out. When we started dating, for the first time in my life, I saw someone who I really, *really* liked. And I didn't want to fuck that up. And then, as I got to know you—and your, like, three boyfriends—I started to get worried about my past."

Jaime seemed taken aback by this, glancing between us. "Peter, you actually felt... ashamed? Damn, girl, you really did make an impression on him."

Alexis was already looking flushed, and at first, I thought it was because of all the sex talk. Then I realized it was a confession she was holding onto. "Well, so, um, yes. I did have just three boyfriends. But that's not…"

Jaime leaned in on her elbows. "The plot thickens."

We both practically heard Alexis's nervous swallow. "I had my own wild time." At first, she wouldn't even meet our eyes. When she did, her blue eyes shined. "Maybe not quite like yours, you two sluts, but let's just say my number wasn't three."

"How many?" Alexis asked. She was enraptured.

"Nothing too crazy?" Her face was so red. "But… I also share Taylor Swift's favorite number."

"What?" Alexis was a closet Swiftie, but I didn't know much.

"Thirteen, you goof," Jaime said. Then, turning to Alexis, brows raised, she repeated, "Thirteen? That's, like, over ten extra guys."

I was hard beneath the dining table.

"Yeah." She looked at me sheepishly.

"Time-out. I seem to recall you telling me that Jaime counted as an ex. How are these ten other guys excluded from your list?"

"Well…" She was bright red. "You two did it more than once…" The implication was clear. She'd had ten one-night stands. That was hot as hell. She went on. "That thing I told you about, the hookup in the club bathroom? I wasn't dating that guy."

"You fucked someone in a club?" Jaime said. "I'm suddenly rethinking the whole suburban wife, girl-next-door thing you've got going on."

"I was young and pretty stupid."

Jaime nodded. "Think we can all make that claim. But also, we had some fun."

"We did."

Jaime met my eyes, and I knew what she was going to suggest before the words were formed. I wanted to stop her. I knew this was trouble. But I also wanted to see where trouble could take us. "How about you let me take your wife out tonight? There's this club I've really wanted to hit up while I'm out here."

Each time my heart pulsed, it felt like someone was slamming a drum against my temples.

"It's up to Alexis," I found myself saying. I was suddenly a college kid again, hanging out with Jaime, feeling reckless and shamefully invulnerable. I just went with it, looking over at my wife, who was taking it all in with a curiosity that only made me harder.

"What do you say, Alexis? It's been a while since I've had a wing woman as hot as you. We could get into some real trouble. And the best part? Peter would be into it."

Alexis and I never took our eyes off of one another, and a whole conversation passed between us.

You sure?

I am.

I'm tempted.

I know you are, and I love it.

Alexis shifted as I gave her a short nod.

"What do you say, Peter? Give her a hall pass for the night? You know you want to."

I do want to. I thought it, and Alexis saw that thought in my face, in the intake of breath, in the blush that worked its way up my neck.

"And don't say you don't have anything to wear." Jaime seemed to have the ability to read our thoughts just as well as we did. "I've got you covered, girl. You may have bigger tits, but my dresses are designed to stretch."

———

"Are you *sure* you're sure?" Alexis asked for the tenth time.

"God, you're sexy." She was standing before the mirror,

rocking a tight black dress that was both way shorter and way lower cut than anything I had *ever* seen Alexis wear. "Have your legs always been that long?"

The dress was Jaime's, but the heels were her own, and I always loved how good she looked in them.

She tugged at the short hem of the dress, but all that did was push her tits together and present even more skin up top. I moved up behind her, running my hand along her body. "Tell me about your hookup in the club."

Alexis stopped fussing with the dress and met my eyes in the mirror. "You're serious?"

"Very much. About all of it. Jaime wasn't lying. I loved watching her with other guys. That look of pure ecstasy on her face when I watched her let go with someone else... I don't think I ever wanted her more."

"So you sometimes watched?"

"I did. Those were some intense times." I put my arm around Alexis, feeling her flat stomach as my eyes roamed her body in the mirror. Her nipples were stiff, poking through the dress. "So tell me about your hookup."

"Right, okay." She fussed with her bangs, brushing the golden sweep to the side. "It was spring break, senior year of college. We were in New Orleans, hitting the clubs, sunbathing at the rooftop pools. You know, just having fun. But we were also staying together in a few hotel rooms, so no real action, and I was getting horny."

"Wait, senior year... weren't you dating that guy? Dave?"

She looked sheepish. "Yeah..."

"Okay, just checking."

"So, um, we were out dancing on the third night, and I met this really hot guy, Andre. He was checking me out. I was giving him the eyes. As soon as he came over, I knew I was going to fuck him. Problem was, I wasn't going back to some guy's place in a strange city, and I couldn't take him back to the room that I was sharing with three other girls..."

"So you improvised." I cupped her tits, squeezing them, feeling her hard nipple.

"This is what happens when I get all worked up with no place to release it."

"You become a cheating slut."

I ran my other hand down between her legs. The hem of her dress was cut higher in the front, showing even more of her thighs.

"Peter, I've never cheated on you. I swear, by the time we met, I got all that out of my system."

I believed her and was grateful for that. But I was also ready for her to revisit that old self later tonight. All it would take was to get her riled up just a little more. "So you dragged Andre into the bathroom."

"He actually gave me the opening." She looked at me nervously again. "He asked if I wanted to do some coke. I knew that meant privacy, so I agreed."

"Wait. Coke?"

Alexis's embarrassed grimace was totally incongruous with her dress, her makeup, her heels. "Yes? It wasn't, like, a habit or anything."

I had heard Alexis tell our kids point blank that she'd never done drugs, not even pot, and only had one cigarette in her life. I'd also believed her because it made sense with the woman I met.

"It was all over the place in college. I didn't do it much, but, you know... guess I'm not as innocent as you thought."

"No, and that's sexy as hell. I'm just surprised, is all. I seem to recall you turning down a joint at some party we went to."

"I don't like smoking. I've actually never tried it."

"But you went into the bathroom with some guy to do some rails."

"I'm full of contradictions. The girls and I had already pre-partied, so it wasn't that big a deal. And as I said, it was more of an excuse."

"But you still did it?" I don't know why, but it was hot as hell getting this insight into the woman I always assumed was a goody-two-shoes.

"Yeah. We did a couple lines on the bathroom sink. Then he bent me over the same sink, pulled my dress up, and fucked me from behind as we…" She grinned at my reflection. "…stared at each other in the mirror. I never saw him again after that."

I paused just before my hand pushed all the way up between her legs. "You're a wild one, Alexis. I love it."

"Not really. Definitely not anymore. Even for me, that was crazy."

"Then it's a good thing we have my good friend, Jaime, to help you out tonight."

She turned, put her hands on my shoulders, and asked one final time. "Are you absolutely sure, like *sure sure* that you're sure?"

I kissed her, long and slow and deeply. "I've never been more sure." Slapping her ass, I stepped back. "Now go and have some fun. And the best part?"

"What's that?"

"You don't have to get nasty in the bathroom. We have a whole house for that."

———

Alone in the house, knowing that the love of my life—the woman I'd spent nearly a third of my life with—was out partying in a dress that screamed sex gave me the biggest buzz that I've had in years. This helpless feeling was something that I had completely forgotten about, tucked away in the long ago past, never to be retrieved. Until now. Until Jaime came back into our life like a fucking maelstrom.

I knew it was a bad idea to invite her here, mostly because I knew it would lead to this very scenario. She knew me—knew the deepest, darkest parts of me and what made my sexual clock tick.

I still remember our final time together. It was that final week of college, after exams were in, before graduation. I was seeing another girl then, Elizabeth—willowy brunette, crazy hot, but also, as Jaime put it, very 'vanilla.' She was like a proto-version of Alexis, a girl I could see myself marrying and having a family with one day, once I was ready to get married and have a family.

Jaime knew that I wasn't ready for that, but also saw the potential for fun. She came over with some booze and her current boy-toy, Adam. We drank. One thing led to another, and by the end of the night, things would never be the same. I watched Adam fuck Elizabeth to orgasm after orgasm as Jaime sucked my very hard dick. I watched Jaime become the first girl to go down on Elizabeth. And I watched any chance at a future with her disappear.

Not that I was ready for a future with anyone. Not Elizabeth, certainly not Jaime. It was only a few years later, when I met Alexis, that all that changed.

Was I risking it all again? Maybe. I didn't think so, though. Just as Jaime knew that I wasn't ready for life with Elizabeth, she loved Alexis and the life we had. I just had to trust my old friend, as crazy as that sounded.

I hit our basement gym, doing a hard—and lengthy—workout on the Peloton just to keep my mind off of what may be going on. I didn't check my phone until I was off and headed for the shower. There was nothing from my wife or my friend. I didn't check in, and they weren't volunteering anything.

That all changed at about 11 o'clock.

+Jaime

Your wife is like the best wing woman I've ever had. Girl knows how to dance.

There were no photos, no videos, nothing like that. Just the text.

Peter

She can be very helpful like that.

Jaime responded with a laughing emoji.

Jaime

She wants to know if you were serious about the hall pass.

There it was, the text delivered like an erotic thud, like my dick passing into a throat or a mouth suddenly closing around my balls. But I didn't need long to answer. My mind hadn't changed.

+Peter

Yes, I'm serious. As long as she's okay breaking from Taylor Swift's number.

Jaime

Oh, I think she's okay breaking it.

Now a photo did arrive, dark and grainy. They were on the dance floor, Alexis facing the camera, eyes closed, head to one side as she tossed her long, blonde hair. Behind her was another man with one hand on her stomach and another just beneath her tits. He was a black guy, shaved head, clean shaven face, broad shoulders, and he seemed to be whispering something into her ear as they danced.

+Peter

So hot. Be safe!

Jaime

Always. Just like old times. We'll see you later. Try to get some rest!

That was the last thing I heard from either of them. I didn't press. I didn't text back. I tried to keep it cool, jerking it slowly to that one photo that they'd shared until I eventually nodded off to sleep.

I heard the laughter downstairs before I heard the actual door open and close—Jaime's laugh, surprisingly loud for a girl her size. It was late. I must have fallen asleep at some point and was still a little shaky from the sleep.

There was more giggling downstairs, followed by some loud shushing. "We don't want to wake my husband," Alexis said. She wasn't being particularly quiet. "Come on. Let's go out back."

I wiped a hand over my face and tried to wake up. I heard their footsteps move through the house, the fridge clattering open, glass clinking, bottles of beer or wine or water being removed. I was finally able to focus on the clock on the wall. 2:23 am.

That's when I heard it—the deep, resonant voice of a man. "Nice home," he said, his voice low, yet strong enough to carry through the floor and up into my room. "You sure..."

The rest of whatever he was saying was lost as they moved outside. The door closed behind them, and I was no longer even a little sleepy. My pulse was up. My palms were sweaty. I wondered if this was a dream, and as I crept to the window, I tried puzzling out if it was a nightmare or fantasy.

They were outside, on our backyard patio, sitting on the dark wicker furniture and drinking beers. What hit me like a bolt was that there wasn't just one guy sitting out there with them, but two—both looking like CrossFit guys, both twenty years their junior, and both black.

Jaime was sitting in one guy's lap, and judging from how he had his hand wrapped around her slender waist, they'd clearly coupled up. Any doubt of that was obliterated a moment later when she turned her head back and the two started kissing. I had flashbacks to our dating days, to parties where things got way out of hand.

But it was Alexis on the two-seater that commanded most

of my attention. Another guy sat with her, the guy from the photo, leaning in, chatting with her in quiet tones. And she didn't seem nervous or awkward at all. She smiled at him, and was expressive and receptive to his clear flirtations. She didn't blush. She wasn't looking towards the house. If I'd stumbled upon this foursome as strangers, they would have looked like two couples.

Alexis looked amazing, so carefree. Gone were the worries of our day-to-day life. There were no kids to fuss about, no bills to pay, no thought of work the next day. It was like time had turned back, only Alexis was still the confident, sexier version of herself that she'd grown into. She rocked that tight, black dress with its spaghetti straps and all that cleavage like it had been tailor-made for her.

The guy chatting with her seemed to appreciate it. She seemed to appreciate him, too—shaved head, cleanly shaved face, a crisp, white collared shirt that contrasted with his dark skin. The short sleeves seemed to strain around his biceps as he raised the bottle of beer to his lips and sipped.

When he pointed out Jaime and his buddy on the chair, still locking lips, Alexis didn't blush or grow flustered. She simply smiled and nodded. My breath caught as she reached out and touched his jaw, her wedding band catching in the starlight as she turned his head to hers.

At this point, finally, as the guy leaned in for the inevitable, she diverted her eyes past him, up toward the windows. Up towards me. Our eyes locked, if only for a moment. Her lips curled into a smile just as she shut her eyes and accepted the lips of another man on hers.

It was one of the most powerful shocks to my system that I've ever felt. Nothing that I'd ever done with Jaime when we were younger compared to seeing my wife and life partner kiss another man. And that look she gave me, just before doing it? It was the last time she looked my way the rest of the night. If I had a problem with what was going on, I'd come down and say it.

I unlatched the window, pushing it open. The night was still, and they were close enough that I could just hear the sounds of kissing—Alexis's kissing. She was really going at it now, and the guy with her had his hand threaded through her pale locks of hair as they got even closer.

On the other chair, Jaime was fully straddling the other guy's lap. He'd lifted her dress so he could grope her thong-clad ass, and she'd pulled the top down to give him access to her tits. Her moans finally drew the attention of Alexis and her guy. They broke their kiss, Alexis glancing over her shoulder to watch.

Her man ran a hand from her knee up the inside of her thigh. I watched that journey more than whatever Jaime was doing. I'd seen that plenty of times, but I'd never seen my wife in this kind of situation. She didn't stop the hand, and as she felt his touch reach the high hem of her dress, she turned to look at him again. Here was her chance to tell him no, to extract herself from this wild time and come back upstairs. Instead, she leaned in and kissed him again, parting her thighs just enough to give him access.

I knew as soon as he found her pussy. She broke the kiss and gasped. Her fingers tightened on the bare scalp of the guy as she held her forehead against his. They were talking, whispering something to one another that I couldn't hear. She gave a short nod, then reached down with her free hand and touched the front of his pants.

No, not just touched—she unzipped, she unbuttoned, she groped inside. With a wiggle, his slacks were open, and she was fishing out a very large, very hard, very black dick. Alexis seemed taken aback by what she was feeling, breaking her gaze from him to stare down between his legs. From my perch at the window, I could see that she couldn't get her fingers to fully wrap around the thing.

Alexis hesitated only a second longer, chewing on her lower lip as she slowly pumped that thick cock. Then I watched as her head descended into his lap, as she held his dick steady, as her lips encircled his cockhead.

I nearly came watching that, despite only barely touching myself. Watching Alexis's cheeks cave in as she sucked another man was almost too much to handle. I faded away from the window, quietly, slowly, and paced around the back of the bedroom to calm myself. My dick wouldn't be calmed.

I grabbed a wad of tissues to manage the inevitable, then retrieved a stool from our utility closet. I carried it back to the window, making sure to sit far enough away that they couldn't see my movements. I really didn't need to be so careful. No one down there was looking up here.

Jaime was on her knees, her head bobbing between her man's knees. Her dress was gone, leaving her in nothing but her thong and her heels. The guy was equally naked, his fit body glistening in the moonlight as he leaned back in his chair and enjoyed the blowjob.

Alexis was still blowing her guy, who'd unbuttoned his white shirt, but otherwise left it on. Her tiny, black dress was still largely intact, but I knew that wouldn't last much longer.

I peeled down my pajama pants and boxers as I watched the scene unfold, my breathing labored, my mind dizzy with this state of dreamy *deja vu*. I'd been here many times before, but many years ago, with a different blonde putting on the show, a different woman ready to lose herself to some guy, knowing that I was watching.

I could just make out the choking from below as both Jaime and Alexis worked more of those big cocks into their throats. Alexis's guy made sure to keep her hair from her face so he could watch. I got to watch, too, in all its vulgar glory.

"Fuck, you're so big," she said, pulling away. Her voice was hoarse from all the sucking. I had to swallow my own groan.

"You like it, don't you." Not a question.

"It's been a while since I've had one so big."

"You've had black dick before?"

Alexis kissed down the shift, lapping at his balls. "Yes."

That thundered through me. She'd never admitted that, but then again, I'd never known about the ten other guys. "It's okay, don't be shy. You like black dick."

"That's... I'm not..."

"It's okay, baby. I like white, married pussy. Particularly blondes. Blondes are definitely the most fun."

As if to demonstrate, Jaime was lowering herself onto the other guy's condom-sheathed cock, facing outward. Even Alexis caught the last bit of that big dick slipping into my old friend's bare-shaven pussy.

The guy with Alexis produced a square condom wrapper from his breast pocket. "Let's do it."

I had to take my hand off my cock as Alexis sat up and pulled off her dress. She wore a strapless, black bra and thong, both of which she stripped off as she stood before this younger, naked man in our backyard.

Alexis was exquisite in her full-frontal nudity—her hips, her tits, her thigh gap, and the musculature of her long, long legs. The young guy sitting on the two-seater, rolling a condom down his gargantuan dick, was just as mesmerized as I was.

He held his hand out, and when she accepted it, he guided her to the spot beside him. It gave me the perfect angle to watch her spread her legs, resting one on the armrest, exposing her bald snatch. I watched as the guy braced himself with a hand on her shoulder, his other on her knee. Alexis guided his swollen dick right up against her, her eyes shifting from his cock to his face.

That look, that exchange, felt like a lightning bolt striking my spine. I shuddered, nearly losing it. The guy pressed his hips forward and sank into her pussy. The rest was lost from view, but I didn't need to see more. It was all there in the way Alexis arched her back and accepted this new dick.

What a fucking sight. For all the playing that Jaime and I had done, we'd never explored the interracial thing. Now it was happening right below me, and it was amazing. Jaime came in a squealing mess in the guy's lap, who apparently filled his condom with come, but it was Alexis who I couldn't take my eyes off of.

The guy was giving it to her hard, his muscular body undulating into her pale, splayed form. His powerful buttocks thrust and tightened with each drive, the movement hammering home that it wasn't *me* hammering her—that she'd be forever changed from here on out. It would be a long time before I'd be able to fuck her without her thinking of how this guy stretched her, how he made her feel things that I just couldn't.

And she was into it. She gave everything to the forbidden sex. She clawed at his shoulders, groped at that thrusting ass, kissed him sloppily when he leaned into her. This was what I loved about watching Jaime fuck other men all those years ago—I loved how turned on she got, how totally fulfilled she was. With Alexis, it was so much more powerful.

Dark skin glistening with sweat, the guy finally finished, flooding his condom with one final, hard thrust forward. Alexis nearly crawled up the back of the wicker sofa as she came with him.

When he pulled free, she was a flopping, gasping mess. She couldn't seem to open her eyes as she ran her fingers through her damp, blonde hair.

I caught a glimpse of her pussy as the guy staggered back, still stretched by her new lover's enormous dick. Then Jaime crawled onto the seat beside her and ran her hand over Alexis's arm. "You're so sexy," I heard her say. "Do you mind if I taste you?"

Alexis snapped out of her hazy euphoria, her eyes wide,

her blush deep. She'd never been with another woman and had always laughed when I'd suggested it. So it was a total surprise when she reached out and drew Jaime in for a soft kiss, then slowly nodded.

I watched in shock as Jaime moved down between Alexis's legs, their eyes fixed on one another. Alexis sighed as she felt Jaime's soft cheeks on her thighs, and then was transported when Jaime started to eat her pussy.

I'd watched Jaime do this before. She'd done it with my ex, Elizabeth. She'd done it with other friends. But I never thought that I'd see it happen with Alexis, who's breathy giggle gave way to a louder gasp. "Oh, my… ahh! Ohhh, that feels so… uhhhh…"

"Dayum," the guy who'd fucked Jaime said.

"That is fucking hot," said the other.

They were stroking their cocks, which were already beginning to harden again and were slowly drifting closer to the two girls. Alexis cupped her tits and pinched her own nipples as she had her first girl-on-girl orgasm.

That's when she saw them around her—two black dicks, erect, tempting. Heavy-lidded, she looked drunk on the sex and the moment. She reached out to Jaime's guy, the new dick, wrapped her hand around it, and guided it into her mouth. He was happy to comply, stepping close to let her suck.

She didn't leave the other man out, though, reaching out with her left hand, stroking him. He climbed onto the seat to give her better access, and a moment later, she switched to sucking his cock as she jerked off Jaime's man. And all the while, Jaime remained between her legs, her blonde head bouncing.

Seeing my wife in the middle of all that, the nexus of pleasure, and how turned on she was, turned *me* on. The foursome shifted again. New condoms were rolled on. New pairings were made, only this time, they were all on the loveseat. Alexis's girthy first lover laid Jaime on her back and entered her, as Alexis straddled the other man and experienced yet another new cock.

This time, I got to watch my wife's naked body undulate in a stranger's lap, her ass and back turned to me, his dark dick peeking out as she started her athletic fuck. The guy sucked on her tits, which I knew she loved, as the other man leaned over from Jaime to kiss her on the mouth.

Even above it all, watching, stroking, trying to hold back, I felt for Alexis as they overwhelmed her senses. It spun round and round, that writhing foursome shifting the wicker seat across our patio in their excitement. It strained beneath all the sex. The foursome didn't care. They fucked on, and Alexis's orgasms rolled.

When the guy fucking Jaime pulled out, I had a feeling that things were headed for a thrilling climax. When he pulled the condom off, I *knew* that they were. He sat up on his knees and guided Alexis's head to his cock. She swallowed it immediately, and like that, my wife had two dicks in her at once.

Jaime wasn't one to be left out. She zeroed in on Alexis's tits, and incredibly, I watched my wife run her free hand down between Jaime's legs and push two fingers inside.

The tangle of bodies barreled to their finish. I wondered who'd get there first.

The answer was me. The orgy was too hot, too wild, too unbelievable to hold off any longer. I came as I watched Alexis start choking on one dick as she began bouncing faster on the other. I came as I watched her press her thumb against my old friend's bare snatch.

The guy with his dick in Alexis's mouth wasn't far behind me. I was still emptying my come into the tissues when he grabbed her head, rammed his cock down her throat, and grunted, "Fuck yeah!" as he shot his load into my wife's willing mouth.

I was just cooling down when he pulled out, leaving Alexis gagging and coughing. Come spilled down her chin. Jaime was there, her lips against Alexis's for a deep, tongue-filled kiss. Alexis returned it with enthusiasm, the two blondes making out until the guy fucking Alexis entered his own endgame. He grabbed her by her heart-shaped ass, flexing those muscular arms, lifting her up and down his dick as he drove his hips up off the cushioned chair.

It was as physical a fuck as I'd ever seen, and one that I don't think I could give to Alexis. This guy man-handled her like she weighed nothing, and Alexis was losing her mind to that feeling.

"Uhn! Uhh! Ahh!"

The two of them came together. She bent her body over him, clutching his head and grinding her hips to take every last inch of black cock inside her. The show was over, at least for me. As I wiped my dick free with the tissues, the last thing I saw was Alexis kissing the man who'd just fucked the shit out of her, a deep sensual and exhausted kiss, a *thank you* kiss, a *that was the best fuck of my life* kiss.

———

Alexis joined me in bed about fifteen minutes later. She was completely naked and looking sheepish as she crept into the dark room. "Are you awake?"

"Of course," I said.

"You… watched?"

I heard the nervousness in her voice. "Hottest thing I've ever seen. Like, ever."

I watched her silhouette relax; her shoulders lose their tension. She crawled into bed with me. I could smell the sex on her, as well as what must have been the heavy cologne of those two guys. "You're not angry?"

"You know I would have come down there if I was."

"Yeah."

"It was amazing watching you down there. You looked so… into it."

She averted her eyes. "I'm sorry."

"Don't be. Never be. Seeing you just give yourself to the moment was the best part." I pulled her to me and kissed her. One thing led to another, and soon she was clawing at my boxers. "Are you too sore?"

"I'll manage," she said as she lowered herself onto me. I slotted right in. She was definitely loosened up from having those larger dicks. We groaned together as Alexis established a slow rhythm.

"I like that you were up here," she whispered. "Watching."

"I liked watching, too." Like a flash, I saw her straddling one man as she sucked the other's cock. My dick swelled inside of her. "I can't believe you did that."

"I can't, either."

"I'm glad you did."

She nuzzled her forehead along mine. "Me too."

She rode me quietly, each of us enjoying the moment of reconnection. I used to love these moments with Jaime, but they never felt so profound as this did now. With her, we just had fun recounting our exploits. With Alexis, she was there to remind me that the most important thing was *us*.

"Are we good?" I thought about Elizabeth, and how that foursome had ended whatever it was we had.

"You tell me," she responded.

"I know that I am, as long as you are. That was all fun down there, but this…" I touched her. "This is what matters most."

"Yes," she sighed. "Yes, all of that."

"So, since we're good… want to do it again?" I asked.

She considered her reply before speaking. I appreciated that. "I don't want to make it a regular thing."

"No, let's not do that."

"And I don't want it to even become, like, our only thing." She kissed my neck, pressing her lips to my ear. "But yes, I want to do it again."

I came with the confession. It was all the reassurance that Alexis needed. She wanted it. I was into it. And our adventures were far from over.

I still had so many questions. What were the guys' names? How did they meet? How did she feel about Jaime going down on her? Or having two dicks in her? Or being with a black man? But all those would have to wait. There would be time to explore them all. There would be time to revel and relive.

"You know," Alexis said with a twinkle in her eyes. "We have two glorious weeks without the kids, and with Jaime still in the house."

"Not so upset anymore?" I said with a chuckle.

"I've come around on it."

"You're still the best wife, though."

"Oh, I know." She kissed me, and started to get out of bed. "And now, I'm going to get even *better*. The three of us are going to have a lot of fun…"

Kenny Wright is an erotic fiction author who writes the kind of steamy, explicit erotica that he likes to read. He gravitates to romantic erotica with themes that tackle extramarital adventures, hotwives, humiliation-free cuckoldry, voyeurism, and the loss of innocence. He's been publishing books since 2012, but has been writing far longer than that. He believes in a world where men read and appreciate erotica, and hopes to contribute to it word by word. Follow him on Twitter at @kennywriter, and find more of his books at kennywriter.com/books.

HER BEST FRIEND'S HUSBAND

Kirsten McCurran

I'm busy stirring the meatballs in the slow cooker for tonight when I hear Rick mumble a curse after he receives a text. I glance over and see him fire off a reply. My first thought is I hope they aren't calling him in to work. Rick doesn't have a choice about going in when they're short-handed at the firehouse.

"Boris and Dina are out for tonight. She's stuck working a double because her relief didn't come in. Boris is just going to stay home," Rick says.

"I bet it was that bitch, Kendra. She's always calling out. I think they'd fire her if we weren't already so shorthanded." Dina and I are nurses at the same hospital. We've been best friends since nursing school.

"He didn't say, just said Dina will probably be stuck there all night."

"He's right. They aren't getting someone else to come in and relieve her on short notice on a Saturday night. That sucks. I feel her pain. I'll text her. But tell Boris to come over anyway."

"Really? You think?"

I'm surprised Rick sounds surprised. "Dina doesn't need to be here for Boris to hang out. He's over all the time."

"That's if we're watching a game or just back from hoops. Saturday nights are a couples' thing."

"I wish Dina was coming over, so I won't have to put up with you two lunkheads on my own, but it'll be fine. Boris doesn't have to stay home alone on a Saturday night because that bitch Kendra would rather go out and party."

"Are you sure, hon? It won't be weird?"

"Not for me. What girl wouldn't want two hunky fire-fighters all to herself? Is it weird for you if your wife hangs out with the boys?"

"Of course, not. I just thought you'd be bored. Are we going to play a game with just the three of us?"

I set the spoon down and replaced the lid over the meat-balls before turning on Rick with my fists on my hips. "I'm getting the feeling you think I'm boring."

Rick leaves his phone on the kitchen island and pulls me tight against him. The heat of his body makes me squirm from the tickle down below I always feel when we're this close. It can be a problem, our chemistry. My husband towers over me and I'm on the tall side at five-eight. He's a big man, a head taller than me with a broad, hard chest under his t-shirt and arms like tree trunks. Rick is the stereotype of the hot fireman. It's no wonder I was in lust at first sight that night in the ER. Love quickly followed.

"Serena, my darling, you are anything but boring. Never have been, never will be. I knew it was you the second I saw you."

I laugh and touch his chest, tracing my fingers over Rick's broad pecs and out to his biceps. I'll never get tired of how sexy my husband is—he couldn't be more different from my first husband—but I can't let him get too big of a head.

Rick has always sworn it *was* love at first sight for him, but I'm pretty sure it was lust on his side too. Is it immodest to admit I know I'm hot? I won the genetic lottery with that rare combination of jet-black hair, porcelain skin, and crystal-blue eyes. People have told me how pretty I am from a young age, especially older men who paid creepy attention much too early. I've always been active and physical, and my body snapped right back after both kids. Keeping that body requires more effort in my forties, but I think I'm more toned than ever because of that. I can't take it for granted anymore.

"I know how you firefighters are, babe. You guys flirt with all the pretty nurses. I was just dumb enough to say yes, and the rest is history."

"I was in too much pain that night to flirt. I think it was all you."

I caress the long scar on his forearm. Rick says he loves that scar because it's a permanent reminder of the night we met. He was brought in over his strenuous objections when he caught the wrong end of a fully involved car fire. The tough guy swore he was fine even though he was trying to hack up a lung from smoke inhalation and his arm was an angry red burn. He dropped his guard and showed vulnerability when I forced him to take oxygen. Seeing the little boy behind the big, strong man was my first clue that Rick might be the one.

"I don't flirt with patients, which you should be very happy about, I might add. And are you *ever* in too much pain to flirt?"

Rick flashes that roguish smile. "I don't know, hon, but I do know I'm not in any pain right now." He boosts me up onto the countertop like I'm featherlight. I love his strength. My legs fold around him when he gives me a long, slow kiss that's hotter than the bubbling slow cooker beside me. "And you're free to flirt as long as you remember who you belong to."

I laugh in between teasing him with flicks of my tongue. He always tells me he's secure enough to let me flirt. Sometimes, I think he even likes it. "This isn't flirting. And I don't belong to anyone, stud."

"I'm pretty sure I'm owning you when you're howling my name." His hands slide under my butt, and we're snug enough that I feel the sizable bulge in his jeans press into my rapidly heating center.

"My pussy maybe." My tongue surges into his mouth and Rick surges between my thighs. I swear I feel him throb and I groan into our kiss.

"As long as I get the good parts, I'm cool with that." There's that grin that's made every woman he's ever met swoon.

"You're ridiculous."

"Tell me that in five minutes."

Rick plucks open the buttons down the front of my tight, white, ribbed cardigan, exposing creamy cleavage. My long, raven hair is swept aside, and he nuzzles me. He's nibbling that special spot behind my ear that guarantees I'll let him fuck me right here on the counter when the timer goes off. I try to push him away, but Rick is insistent. He's subtly massaging one of my breasts and his breath on my neck makes me crazy. This man knows how to push my buttons, but if I don't get the roasted eggplant out of the oven the kitchen will fill with smoke. You'd think a firefighter would appreciate that.

"I have to get that before it burns," I insist.

"I'm already burning for you, Serena."

I laugh and reach for the spoon beside me. Rick shouts and relents when I dab a spot of red sauce from the meatballs on his cheek. "Get away from me, you cheeseball!" I hop off the counter. I'll button my sweater after I rescue the eggplant.

The oven door is barely open when Rick is right behind me, pressing into my butt when I bend over to pull out the cookie sheet. His excitement grinds hard into my round behind. I have to pause and fight the urge to let him drag my jeans down right there.

I didn't realize I was so wet until I felt the promise of having his thickness inside me. I almost don't blame him because my ass looks pretty fantastic in these jeans. I only wore them because I didn't want my man distracted by Dina's juicier ass. Rick makes it worse when he presses a hand between my thighs and makes me swoon. He must feel the damp heat, even through my jeans.

"You have to stop, Rick. This is going to burn," I whine, torn. *Let it burn!* No one's coming over now anyway.

"I don't care."

Rick unbuttons my jeans and I find my last reserve of willpower. I am not going to let the eggplant that I took time to slice and season burn, just so I can get my cheap thrills. And I thought Boris was going to come over anyway. I give Rick a teasing wiggle of my butt and bump him away with it. He grunts with frustration. I rescue the eggplant.

"Did you text Boris and tell him he's still welcome?"

Rick waits for me to set the cookie sheet on top of the stove before pawing me again. He's only successful because I truly love it when it paws me. It could be my favorite thing. But this is not a time for pawing. I need to finish cooking and he needs to text his friend. I let him massage my breasts before pushing his hands out of my sweater because I know I'm getting more out of it than he is. I grab Rick through his jeans, and he gets weak in the knees when I knead it. I'm in control now.

"Do what I told you, and maybe I'll reward you later," I tease.

"Reward me now. If I don't text Boris, you can reward me all night. Doesn't that sound like more fun, hon?" He grunts when I squeeze him harder. It might hurt if his jeans weren't in the way. The protection just makes it feel good.

"I didn't go to all this effort to let it all go cold while you drag me upstairs like a caveman. Text Boris, or I will. And if I have to do it, I just might forget to button my sweater back up."

Rick chuckles. "Fine, I'll do it, but only because I know you're super horny now and you're going to fuck me silly the second he leaves."

"We'll see." My smile tells him he's right.

His phone is in his hand, and he snaps a photo of my sweater hanging open before I can react. I pull it closed three seconds too late.

"You'd better delete that."

"Hey, I have to convince Boris to come over some way."

"You wouldn't dare."

Rick's charming smile is more of a smirk now. "And you wouldn't leave your sweater unbuttoned when he comes over."

"Is that a challenge? I flash Boris like this, or you show him the picture anyway?"

"Now that's a fun game to play tonight! I think you got me back on board for game night, Serena."

"Don't push me," I threaten, like we're seriously playing a game of chicken with my tits.

Rick knows I'd never flash my best friend's husband, even in a bra. It's a sexy, lacy bra. I'm just as sure Rick wouldn't text a picture of my tits hanging out to his best friend—at least I think I'm sure he wouldn't. He does love to push my buttons almost as much as he likes to show off his toys, like his jacked-up truck in the driveway—not that I'm one of Rick's toys. Not until later tonight after Boris leaves anyway.

"I'll text him now, and you'll just have to wonder what I send."

"Do whatever you want." I try to sound like I don't care. "Just keep in mind you'll have to deal with Dina at some point."

Rick wanders off with his phone. He's not going to do it.

No way. Right? I'm sure he won't, but why do I get a little shiver of excitement thinking he just might?

———

I realize just before Boris arrives that I should have let Rick fuck me. My thirst for my husband does not slake with the passage of time. I watch him through the patio doors, preparing a fire in the pit for later, and I only want him more. The black t-shirt looks like it was painted onto his broad chest. His jeans might do more for his ass than the ones I'm wearing do for mine. I'm tempted to go out there and blow him right on the patio. I'd stop short of letting him come just so he's as horny as I am—if I could control myself.

It's been too long since we had sex out on the patio. It's only a possibility on the weekends my ex has the kids, and Rick is off, which has not coincided often enough lately. Rick was right. We should have let Boris stay home and Rick could have ravaged me all night.

I have to get the door, of course, even though I'm busy in the kitchen and Rick is in one of our deck chairs drinking a beer. I swear he's perfected his *I can't hear the door* act. I smile to hide my frustration and greet Boris at the door with our customary exchange of a hug and a kiss on the cheek. He towers over me like my husband, but otherwise, the two men are complete opposites.

Rick is fair-haired and clean-shaven. An all-American boy, he could replace Chris Evans in *Captain America* if they wanted to go ten years older. Boris has thick black hair and a beard that make him look like a pirate. The bearded look doesn't usually do it for me, but he makes it work. I understand why Dina hasn't made him shave it. Both of his arms are also full sleeves of tattoos, as is most of his back when his shirt is off. A lot of his tats incorporate Cyrillic words that give him a sexy air of danger—not that I'd ever confess that to Dina or my husband. Boris could be one of those anonymous villains in a *John Wick* movie. Rick only has one tattoo, a red Maltese Cross with the number of his Hook and Ladder company. I love that my man is sort of like an overgrown Boy Scout. A very sexy, overgrown Boy Scout.

"Thanks for still inviting me, but you guys didn't have to have me over tonight. I could have just gone to the bar and watched the game."

I rub his shoulders, which are just as strong and maybe a smidge broader than Rick's, and say, "Don't be silly. You're always welcome here. Dina wouldn't forgive me if I let you starve anyway. We don't need her here to have fun, right?"

"I wouldn't tell her that." Boris smiles, but sometimes I think he's afraid of my little flame-haired best friend, even though he's twice her size. I understand why. Dina can be scary.

"I have more sense than that. Come on in. Rick is out back. I can grab you a beer from the fridge, or whatever. Feel free to eat now if you're hungry."

"Whatever you made smells wonderful, but I'd better go out and see Rick before he thinks I've disappeared somewhere with his wife."

"He knows I'm perfectly safe with you because again, your wife is scary and would murder you if you laid a hand on me—and me too for letting it happen."

Boris laughed. "Yeah, if we ever sneak off, we'll need to make sure Rick and Dina are distracting each other."

All of us harmlessly flirt all the time. We're quite the tight foursome. Dina and I have been besties since we met in nursing school before I had kids, and she was burning her way through every hot guy she met. I'm not a shrinking violet, but I don't have her nerve and always secretly admired her ability to just tell a hot guy, "Let's fuck." Rick and Boris have been best friends since the firefighter academy and still work in the same house. I introduced Dina and Boris after I met Rick. I thought my petite friend would have fun climbing all over Rick's tall, dark, and handsome friend. I had no idea Boris would be the last stop on Dina's fun train.

The boys hang out on the patio, and I prepare two heaping plates for them. I made enough food for an army, but there were supposed to be four people, and the boys have huge appetites, and I knew most of it would be for them. I probably shouldn't wait on them, but I'm old fashioned that way. I like serving my man—or men, tonight. And I love that Rick appreciates it, unlike my ex who just took advantage. My husband makes me feel adored in a way no other man ever has.

"Wow, Serena, you've outdone yourself. This eggplant is amazing," Boris marvels.

"I only seasoned it and threw it in the oven." I laugh and enjoy the compliment. I've joined them out on the patio. The early spring evening is unusually warm, but I'll still need to throw something over my sweater if Rick doesn't start the fire soon.

"Yeah, you don't need to fawn all over her like you're trying to get laid," Rick says.

"Old habits die hard," Boris replies.

"Did you guys still want to play a game?" I ask, between bites. I'm trying to eat a meatball sandwich as ladylike as possible, without dripping sauce onto my white sweater.

"Why not?" Rick answers. He's tearing into his without a thought. Sauce smears on his chin. "Do you have anything in mind?"

"I think a lot of the games we usually play, like Cards Against Humanity, require four people. We could try one of those, or we could fall back on one of the kids' games if you guys are feeling silly."

"I'm good with whatever. I'm just happy to tag along."

"There's always strip poker," Rick suggests. He suggests it every time we get together for game night.

"Are you hoping we're going to eventually say yes?"

I realize there's no *we* when it comes to women tonight with no Dina here and my husband's suggestion sounds more dangerous when it's just me with two men.

"He's always hoping that. My man Rick just likes seeing naked women," Boris says.

"He can see me naked anytime he wants."

"Good point. I guess that means he's usually trying to see Dina naked. I should probably be jealous." Boris shrugs and sips his beer.

"Me too, but I've probably seen Dina naked almost as much as you have and I see his point," I reply.

"I'd like to hear more about that," Boris says.

"Sorry to kill your fantasies, but when we've changed in front of each other before going out, stuff like that. No naked pillow fights." I laugh.

"Haha, but you can't kill my fantasies, Serena. They'll always be there."

"I admit to nothing, but if I was trying to see Dina naked, I'm sure Boris wants to see you naked just as badly," Rick interjects.

Boris doesn't even pretend he's not checking me out— especially my tight sweater. "What guy wouldn't? But I'm not the one who always suggests strip poker."

"The two of you better simmer down or I'm going to tell Dina you were trying to get me naked while she wasn't here."

Boris chuckles. "She does have major FOMO. She hates being left out."

"I'll make you a deal, babe. If you ever convince Dina to play strip poker or any other strip game, we'll do it."

"I think you forget how persuasive I can be," Rick threatens.

"Good luck with that." My best friend has a wild side, but I think her strip poker days are behind her now that we're both in our mid-forties. I know mine are. "Now what do you really want to play?"

————

Cards Against Humanity has always been one of our go-to games when we're feeling silly and don't care who wins—not that we're ever uncompetitive. We're always a competitive bunch. Each one of us tries to come up with the most outrageous answers. Outrageous usually means dirty in our group.

Dina has the filthiest mind among us, and Boris loves to play along. I like to think I'm right there with her, but I have limits and Dina has none. Rick leans into his all-American boy image and tends to be more reserved, but I know that man better than anyone. My husband is secretly as dirty as the rest of us. He's just not comfortable letting his freak flag fly in front of others.

Rick starts the fire and our threesome gathers around it on our comfy patio furniture. Orange-cushioned rattan furniture surrounds the firepit, with loveseats on each side. I take the chaise end of ours—I deserve to kick back after doing all the cooking—and Rick is on the far end, with a space between us where our cards sit.

Boris takes the loveseat to Rick's left. He looks lonely over there without Dina by his side. She's missed, but we get plenty raunchy without her. Boris seems to be making up for her absence. I swear he somehow ended up with every dick card in the deck. I can't help laughing when he plays *A bigger black dick* and *Third base* in response to my *For my next trick, I'll pull a [blank] out of my [blank]?* card. This is after he responded to me pulling *Why am I sticky?* with *A bigger black dick.*

"I'd pay money to see that," Boris says while I laugh. He drinks.

"Would you now? I don't think you have enough money," I reply once I catch my breath.

"I can borrow against my retirement. Dina won't mind."

"How do you know she hasn't already seen that? We used to go out dancing together to pick up boys in our young, wild days, you know."

"If you'd like to share with the group, hon?"

"A girl doesn't share her secrets. Besides, do you really want to hear about how Dina and I picked up a couple of huge Black guys and let them finish all over us?"

I take a long, slow pull of my beer to let him think about that. Strangely, the fire in his eyes makes me think that maybe Rick does want to hear the story. He must know I don't have one. Does he wish I did? I don't think we're drunk, but maybe we've had a few too many beers. I'm in my giggly, teasing stage of drinking.

"Fuck, I do," Boris eagerly answers. Is he cool with his wife taking a load from some rando?

"Sure, go ahead and tell us," Rick says.

My husband just wants to hear how dirty a story I can make up. Dina could reel off the filthiest, porn-worthy story without hesitation. Rick doesn't think I'll do it, which only makes me want to prove him wrong. I don't back down from a challenge, even one like this.

"Well, this one night we went out after work. We did that sort of thing in our twenties, back before we just wanted to crawl into bed and sleep after a long shift. Anyway, we changed into our sluttiest club gear in the locker room. I told you, Boris, I've seen your wife naked as much as you have. Anyway, the guys at the hospital were pretty shocked to see Dina and I out of our scrubs and in these tiny, shiny dresses."

"Oh, was it one of the guys at the hospital, like an orderly, who dragged you guys back to the locker room for a crazy threesome?" Rick sounds a little too excited when he asks.

"First of all, racist much? The Black guy who made me all sticky can't be a doctor? He has to be an orderly? Next, you'll say guys can't be nurses." I stick my tongue out at him.

"Fine, point taken," he concedes.

"I thought you and Dina took loads all over you. Were you the only sticky one?" Boris sounds disappointed.

"One guy only has so much to give, but Dina would never let me take it all by myself. She'd be too jealous. Stop sidetracking me! This was not the time we had a threesome. Anyway..."

"You guys had a threesome?" Rick asks.

He looks like he wants to pounce on me. I bet he would if Boris wasn't sitting right there. It reminds me of how horny I've been all night. Maybe that's why I'm willing to tell this wild story.

"Not that night. Can I tell my story?" I wait for the boys to nod. "Okay, we went to the club, and I don't think it's immodest to admit we didn't have any trouble getting attention. We let a few guys buy us drinks, but it didn't get them any more than a couple of dances. Dina and I just had fun playing the game. And then these two guys came along." I pause and try to think of what comes next. I reach for an obvious cliché. "They were linemen from the local university."

"Younger guys, hot," Boris says. He sets his beer aside and cracks a fresh one. I've got him on the edge of the seat. The fire dancing in his eyes makes him look eager to hear how dirty I got with his wife.

"Hey, they weren't that much younger. Dina and I were only just out of nursing school. So, we let these guys buy us drinks and they're all over us on the dance floor, and when they ask us back to their place, Dina and I are ready to go."

"Did you guys do it in the dorms?" Rick sounds like he loves the idea. He sweeps the cards off the cushion between us and snuggles close. His warmth is nice. I'm getting chilly, even with the fire.

"Is it hotter if we fucked them on their bunk beds in their dorm room?" I swear he almost licks his lips and I giggle.

Rick is too easy, but that's part of why I love him. "Sorry to disappoint you, but these guys were seniors. They took us back to their off-campus apartment."

"Two hot, young nurses. Two stud college football players. Sounds like the perfect recipe for a wild night. Did they take turns with you, or was it side-by-side?" I start to speak, but Boris interrupts me. He's on a roll. "No, wait. I bet you and Dina were facing each other and making out while they took you from behind. That's it, isn't it?"

I feel Rick pulse against my hip when Boris pitches his crazy fantasy. He's turned toward me, with his arm around my shoulders. My husband *likes* this fantasy that two hot, young guys had Dina and I while we kissed. He probably even imagines them high fiving over us. It's so absurd I laugh. Rick has to know I'd never consider anything like that, but maybe he likes thinking about a version of me that would.

The hard dick pushing into my hip brings my horniness roaring back. Rick's been trying to get into my jeans all night and Boris has been cock blocking him the entire time—either waiting for our friend or because he's here now. It's not Boris' fault Rick and I want to tear each other's clothes off and can't, but I'm about ready to call it an early evening. My silly story might even be getting to me. I think maybe if Rick and I get cozier, he'll take the hint. I pull my husband closer onto the chaise end with me and settle onto his lap with my back to his chest.

"Well, which version do you want it to be, Boris? Are Dina and I making out while these football players screw us silly, or are they switching off and tag teaming us?" I must have had too many beers. I can't believe those words came out of my mouth. Dina would be so proud.

Boris turns it over in his head, trying out both scenarios. I realize our friend is sitting there imagining me getting fucked by some hung stranger and the tingle in my core transforms into a deep throb of need. I know I'm attractive, but I don't go through the world thinking about men imagining me fuck— especially men I know so well. We were in each other's weddings! Boris looks at me over the fire and I wonder, is he picturing me on all fours taking it from behind and sucking on Dina's tongue, or are his wife and I on our backs with our ankles in the air? Why do I want him to be paying more attention to me in that fantasy? I feel a sexual current running between us and I'm uncomfortable because I like it too much.

"It's hotter if they were swapping off," Rick chimes in, his voice husky. His hands rest on my thighs and his erection is pressed firmly between my legs. I swear he's subtly humping my butt. He's as into this as Boris and me.

"Yeah, because when they're done, they can just pull out and make you both sticky," Boris adds, almost moaning the words. He's *definitely* picturing it now.

Dina may be in the fantasy, but my best friend's husband —my husband's best friend—should not be imagining me getting showered with a fantasy man's cum. I shouldn't be either. Guys finishing on me has never been my thing. It's mostly happened because I made them pull out. But seeing it through the guys' eyes tonight has me soaked.

Rick holds my hips and is grinding my butt harder. His motion isn't obvious, but I still can't believe he's doing it in front of our friend. He might make a mess in his jeans. I put my hands over his, but don't move them. It's so wrong, but it feels so right. I check in on Boris and I'm relieved he doesn't appear to realize what's happening over here. What'll happen if he does? I have a wild thought. *Does Boris really want to watch me?* That could never happen. Dina would murder us all. I couldn't fuck my husband while someone watches us anyway. Could I?

"You guys do get this never happened, right? We're just being silly." I want to defuse the situation, but my breathy, uncertain tone charges the night air even more.

"What about that threesome you mentioned?" Boris asks. He's completely focused on me. He must see Rick is grinding me. *Fuck, don't look at us—at me—that way.*

"What threesome?" I ask. The heat building inside makes it hard to think straight. Did I mention a threesome?

"You said that wasn't the time you and Dina had a threesome. When did the threesome happen?" Rick asks.

"Oh, right. Maybe I'm just trying to wind you up."

"I don't think so. Don't leave us hanging, Serena," Boris says.

I need Rick to stop grinding his very hard cock against me because I need to think straight, but all I can focus on is wanting to tear both of our jeans out of the way so he can slip inside me. The thing is, I don't know if I can get away with lying. While Rick and I have never gotten deep into my past, Dina may very well have told Boris everything. He'll likely call me out if I try to fib. He seems like he's waiting for me to try to lie.

Rick has never been one to ask too many questions about my sexual history beyond general teasing about just how wild Dina and I were in nursing school, and I was happy to keep the sordid details from him. I was never as slutty as my friend, but I've done a few things that could make my husband look at me differently. I don't want that.

"We didn't really have a threesome. Things didn't get that far," I evade.

"Serena, you had a threesome, or you didn't," Boris presses.

"Did you and Dina hook up with someone?" Rick asks. I swear his cock surges harder against my butt. "What do you know, brother?"

Boris smirks and sips his beer. "Do you want me to tell it, or do you want to do it, Serena?"

"There's not much to tell," I insist.

"Our girls brought a guy back to Dina's place one night,"

Boris says. He's impatient. "Dina told me he was so hot they just couldn't resist."

"We were very drunk, and Dina insisted. It was more her than me."

"You and Dina fucked some guy together?" Rick sounds stunned. I want to turn around and read his expression, but he holds me firmly in place. He's having too much fun grinding me.

"We did not fuck him together!" I blurt out, and it sounds way more defensive than I planned. "*I* didn't fuck him."

"That's true, at least according to Dina. Serena got cold feet, but she didn't run out of there either. She says you stayed and watched."

"I… Okay, I did. The three of us were fooling around. Clothes were coming off. Things were progressing. I reached my limit and bowed out."

"What was your limit?" Rick asks.

"I…"

"The girls took turns sucking his dick." Boris is all too pleased to answer for me. I've always liked him, but that's changing. What's brought this side out of him?

"Jesus, you did what?" Rick gasps.

"Babe, I didn't…we…"

I try to turn and face him this time, but my husband is forceful. I'm kept in place, but his hands move. They slide to the sliver of exposed skin between my sweater and jeans. His light touch tickles and I squirm. Rick groans when my ass moves against him. Caressing fingers travel up under my sweater. I squirm harder. *Boris is right there. What's he doing?*

"Didn't what? Didn't help Dina suck this guy's dick?" Rick's voice is husky.

"I…I did…a little bit…" The confession warms me even further. My sweater feels so heavy now, especially with Rick's big hands under it. He cups my breasts through my bra, and I whimper. Fuck, I want him. I can't take this torture. Boris has to leave. Or he can sit out here while I drag my husband inside for a hard fuck. I don't care which.

"And then you stayed and watched while Dina fucked the guy, didn't you?" Boris accuses.

I stare daggers at him, but it's meaningless because he's staring back with open hunger. Rick can't like his best friend looking at me like that. Dina would have his balls. Boris keeps staring, willing me to confirm his accusation.

"I did…"

"What else did you do?" Boris leans so far forward he's almost out of his chair.

"I…*I touched myself…*" The words just slip out.

"Jeez, Serena," Rick moans in my ear. He doesn't sound angry.

Rick isn't angry. He's kissing the side of my neck and behind my ear. His lips brush those intimate places that make me tremble and whimper. I close my eyes and revel in the ripples of pleasure flowing through me. He nibbles and I barely swallow my whine. I don't want Boris to see how easy I am when you find the perfect spot on my neck. Rick holds my hips. He's not trying to hide it anymore. He's grinding hard like he can fuck his way right through our jeans.

Fingers pluck at my buttons and my sweater pops open under the strain of my heaving breasts. I'm thrilled to be free but wait—Rick is holding my hips while he dry humps me. *Who…* My eyes flicker open to see Boris kneeling on the chaise beside us, exposing me. I reach for his hands, but my effort is weak, and he brushes me away. His fingers flicker along the lacy edge of my bra. He's lost his mind. We've all lost our minds.

"Boris, you have to stop. We can't do this." I don't even sound like I mean it to myself, but this can't happen. "Rick?"

My husband doesn't pause kissing my neck to answer. He nuzzles deeper into my thick, raven hair. He's not going to rescue me. I can't believe Rick is willing to share me. Where's my all-American man?

"We can't do this to Dina. It's not right. She'll never forgive us."

Boris chuckles. He's lightly massaging my breasts and it's winning me over to his side. His hands are as big and strong as my husband's. I'm being worshipped by two handsome, powerful men. It's hard to resist.

"Only because she's not here. We know she's good with threesomes. She'll just be jealous you're the one getting all the action this time, Serena."

I simply can't believe my best friend would be good with her husband groping my tits. She's not that wild child who lured me into so many risqué nights anymore. We're grown women. We're mothers! I grasp Boris' wrists. I do need sex—badly—but he can't be a part of it.

"We can't do this. We can't all fool around behind Dina's back. Neither of us wants to hurt her," I insist. Even Rick stops when he hears my tone. He knows when I'm serious. My body is throbbing, demanding I surrender, but I've found a reserve of willpower.

"Is it the behind her back part that's bothering you? Are you good if she says it's okay? Rick? Are you good?"

"Apparently, my wife likes threesomes, why not? You're down, aren't you Serena?" His voice is low and dark. I don't even recognize it. What's going on with my husband?

I roll my eyes and snort. These guys are crazy and aren't listening to me. "Fine, if Dina gives her blessing you two studs can do whatever you want with me. It's a shame she's not here to ask."

Boris pulls his phone right out of his hip pocket and dials.

"What are you doing? You can't ask her that! She's at work."

I try to smack the phone away, but Rick restrains my arms.

My own husband is working against me. I can't wait for Dina to put these guys in their place.

"What's up, sexy?" Dina's voice floats from Boris' phone.

"Sorry to bother you, but the three of us are here and things are getting out of hand, and Serena wants your blessing before we keep going."

"I did not ask for your blessing!" I shout.

"What kind of out of hand?" Dina sounds amused.

"The best kind."

Boris turns his phone and I see he's made a video call. Dina's in the nurses' lounge and the lights are low. She smiles when she sees my sweater open and Rick holding my arms.

"Oh, *that* kind of out of hand. I can't believe the three of you would finally do this without me. Very naughty." *Finally?*

"So, can we have fun with Serena, sweetie? I promise I'll make it up to you." Boris turns on the charm big time.

"The three of you can do what you like, as long as I can watch. I'm on an extended break to take a nap, but this is much more fun. I haven't seen Serena get crazy in a long time."

"You know this is insane, right Dina?" I complain.

"It's insane that you're doing it without me. I didn't think you had it in you to instigate this, but I'm proud you're finally letting your inner slut come out to play again."

"I didn't instigate anything!"

"Have fun kids. Just put the phone somewhere so I can see everything. Oh, and you *all* have to make this up to me. All of you owe me for letting you have fun tonight."

What is happening? The world is upside down. Responsible adults don't have threesomes on their patio, and responsible nurses certainly don't watch from work. I must be the only one thinking straight.

Boris uses a pillow to prop up his phone at the far side of the loveseat, where Dina can watch everything. And then he's touching me again, Rick is kissing me again, and I stop thinking straight too. The lips on my neck and the hands all over my body feel so good I realize I'm a fool for resisting this. The boys can have me. I don't want to fight them anymore.

Rick unsnaps my jeans so he can squeeze a hand inside. My soaked panties are plastered to my swollen mound, and he has to peel them away to get his hand in between. I gasp and push at his fingers when they stroke between my folds. Boris sees just how badly I need it, but he could probably tell from the other side of the firepit. He pinches both nipples, and the stinging thrill is just short of pain.

I can't stand the satin and lace barrier between us and lean up from Rick to unhook my bra. Boris kisses me while I'm elevated. I feed him my tongue without thought. My soaring ardor doesn't allow for hesitation. His beard is scratchy on my smooth cheeks. I prefer my husband's smooth face and don't know why Dina doesn't make him shave. I haven't kissed anyone but Rick in nine years. I hold onto Boris and devour him. I hadn't realized how hungry I was for a new experience.

"Damn Serena, your tits are great," Boris says, laying me back against my husband. He sculpts them with his hands and strums the tips with his thumbs. The electricity sparks to my core and it throbs harder.

"Aren't they? I always tell her those are the best tits I've ever seen. I've got the hottest wife out there," Rick confirms. His fingers dig deeper inside me. My hips rock to pull them even deeper.

They're talking about me like I'm an object and I'm tempted to say *I'm right here guys,* but the truth is I'm eating up their praise. The guys make me feel like a queen.

"Except maybe for Dina. Love you, sweetheart." Boris tosses the last part over his shoulder toward his phone.

"Dina's got great tits, too," Rick agrees. I don't love my husband complimenting her breasts when all the attention is supposed to be focused on me, but he's not wrong. I'm lucky to still have full, perfect teardrops in my mid-forties, but Dina's chest is even bigger than mine and that always grabs attention. She's one of the rare women I feel competitive with when I go out.

Boris presses a thumb to my lips, and I stare into his dark eyes while I lick and then suck it. I suck it hard and lick while it's in my mouth. I love how he looks blown away. The guys aren't the only ones who can tease. My lips smack when he pulls his thumb away. He uses the thick, wet digit to slowly rub circles over one of my tight, pulsing tips. I try to keep eye contact when I moan, but it's too much of a tease and my eyes flicker closed. I want to just float on the pleasure. He presses his other thumb into my mouth, and I suck that one too. Boris teases both nipples with his wet thumbs and my chest heaves while I try to keep some semblance of control. Rick must feel my sheath tighten around his fingers.

God, their hands are all over me and I need it so badly I'm shaking. Boris gets rougher with my breasts the more he sees how it turns me on. I'm panting and constantly moaning. I try to push my tits into his hands, but he won't allow it. The boys are in control of my body. Rick curves his fingers inside me and hits a perfect pace.

"Ahhh…ahhh fuck…fuuucckkk…ahhh…"

The climax is so sudden that it takes my breath away. I swear I've been building to it all night. My brain scrambles and I keep coming. It feels like their hands are everywhere on my body. I'm still swirling in my bliss when Boris tugs my jeans down my legs. He pauses to pull off my Uggs—the sexiest part of my outfit—and toss them away. My panties go with my jeans, and I'm left barely wearing my sweater.

"You're beautiful when you come, Serena," Boris says.

"You're amazing, honey. You're so on fire," Rick adds. God, I feel like I'm going to burn up.

Boris kneels at the foot of the chaise and pulls me

forward by my hips. Rick still cradles me, but I'm off him enough that our friend can taste me without being too close to my husband's crotch. Boris pulls my legs over his shoulders and brushes his lips along my damp thighs. His bristly beard tickles and I giggle and squirm even though I'm so aroused.

"Something wrong?" Boris asks, smiling. He keeps brushing me with his beard.

"That tickles!"

I try to close my thighs, but his head is there. Boris plunges in and I'm feeling anything but ticklish. His tongue dives between my folds. I'm so drenched that he slurps when he devours me. My eager hips grind at his mouth. Boris rewards my sluttiness by slipping one—then two—fingers deep inside me. *God yes!* I feel filled and it's just what I needed. Well, not quite. I truly need to be filled by something else.

The next few minutes are heaven. Or it could be an hour. I'm so spoiled by these two hunky firemen that time loses meaning. Boris worships my pussy. Rick massages my breasts and tortures my nipples in that special way only he can. My husband's had years of practice and knows my body so intimately. The guys make me come so easily and I just don't stop. One orgasm rolls through me like a tidal wave and the next is coming before the first subsides. The pleasure is so intense that I can't control my shouting. Rick covers my mouth, which only makes me come harder. At least my shouts are muffled.

"She's a damn hellcat, man. I had no idea," Boris says, looking up from between my thighs. His beard is shiny with the evidence of how hard he's made me come.

"Serena's a fun girl," Rick chuckles, still covering my mouth.

Boris strokes my slick button and I keep trembling and moaning. My eyes are going to roll into the back of my head.

It's almost too much. I wonder if the boys can make me come so much, I pass out.

"Beautiful and sexy. You're pretty perfect, Serena," Boris tells me, his dark eyes searing into mine. He looks like he's contemplating all the dirty things he wants to do to me. Is it disloyal to my husband and best friend that I want him to do them all?

I'm a rubbery, panting mess when the guys reposition me. I shrug my sweater and unfastened bra off somewhere along the way, leaving me nude on the patio. I'm stretched out on the chaise and the guys stand over me. I'm so desperate for it that I don't even consider that our neighbor to the left could look out of a second-floor window and see us. What a scene we would be! Two men stand over my naked body unfastening their pants and deciding who'll do what to me. I can't wait to find out.

"Do you mind if I?" Boris asks, gesturing at me.

"She's my wife. I think I should get to fuck her first. I'd expect the same with Dina."

"Yeah, good point."

"Mmm, don't I get a say?" I ask, writhing enticingly on the chaise.

Rick laughs. "You're going to love whatever we do to you."

"Do you think I'm that much of a slut now?" I ask. The guys laugh. "The two of you at least have to be as naked as I am. We're not doing this with you two Winnie the Poohing this."

They're both still in their t-shirts with their jeans around their ankles. Both men have hot bodies, and I want to see them. Watching them peel off their tight t-shirts is quite the show. Their long, thickly muscled torsos are masculine perfection. I know I should say my husband is sexier, but I'm happy I'm not forced to choose. I tease my slick furrow while

I watch them strip. Their bodies look otherworldly in the flickering orange firelight.

Rick is on me first. He kneels on the chaise between my open legs. His cock pulses with excitement for me. He holds it, but I reach down to grasp it. I need to feel his heavy heat in my hand. I need that thing inside me.

"You're eager for it, hon." His voice is a smooth purr. He needs it as badly as I do.

"I do, babe. I've wanted it all night, but damn it, I need you to fuck me now." My glacial blue eyes flick from my husband to Boris when I say it. They both need to know how badly I want them. The hungry way Boris looks down at me when I say it makes me melt.

I cry out when Rick buries it in me. I'm looking at Boris and don't see it coming. God, it's hot to look into the eyes of one man while another shoves his cock inside you. I'm always so full when Rick is inside me, but Boris made me come so hard that my husband just slips it right in.

"Don't think you've ever been so hot and wet, Serena," Rick grunts, adjusting to my furnace. My chute clings to him, desperate for him to start fucking me. "Boris got you going."

"I bet she's always this hot," Boris says, smiling down at me as he comes closer.

I'm not, but he can't know that. Both guys teamed up on me, but how does my husband feel so drenched after his best friend went down on me? I hope he's not jealous. Rick could have stopped this.

My legs are thrown over Rick's arms, tilting my hips. He has the perfect angle and starts hammering me. *Oh fuck, it's good! Fuck, this is what I needed!* Rick grins at me seeing what a needy slut I am. He loves this. Has he wanted me to be this slutty all these years? Boris smiles too, watching me jolt with every powerful thrust. My raven hair is fanned out under me and my tits bounce. He strokes himself while he watches, and drips with excitement. I want that cock.

Boris kneels by my head and feeds it to me. He smears his dripping arousal over my lips, and I lick them. I look at my husband while I do it. He's smiling. He truly does love my sluttiness. Boris cradles my head, tilting it, and feeds me. He's every bit as big as my husband—maybe even thicker. I open wide, my lips stretch, but I still strain to accept him. He doesn't force it, but he's firm, pushing deeper until he hits the back of my throat. My lips are already tight around him, but that's when I really start sucking.

"That's it, sweet Serena, suck that cock like you're starving for it. That's a hot fucking mouth," Boris moans. His fingers tighten in my hair. Does my husband mind him talking to me like this? I'm not ashamed to admit I love it.

"She loves sucking cock, man. Couldn't get enough when we first started dating," Rick grunts between pumps. He's riding me harder watching his friend use my mouth. I guess he doesn't mind how Boris is speaking to me.

"Let's see if you can get it down your throat, Serena. Can you do that for me, sweetie? Open wide and relax. Yeah… *fuck*…that's good sweetie…*fuck that's good cock sucking…*"

I take Rick into my throat, but I'm always in control to make sure I don't gag. The boys have full control over my body. I'm just being used—at both ends. Boris pulls my hair and I thrill. He shanks his meat deep into my throat and it burns. I feel like I'm going to suffocate on his cock, but he pulls back when my face turns red. It's only a brief respite. Boris pushes back into my throat and keeps going. His heavy, shaved balls brush my cheek. I'm proud, even though I have tears in my eyes.

Everything is a blur after that. Rick's fingers dig into my thighs, and he pounds me harder than he ever has before. He finds a new gear watching Boris fuck my throat. I try sucking, but my brain is scrambled. Rick's punishing cock pushes wave after wave of ecstasy through me. Boris steadily, relentlessly plunges my throat, using my mouth like a sex toy. He uses my mouth even when I'm screaming my orgasm through his cock. I think he likes the way that vibrates it.

I'm still moaning when they both pull out of me. Neither of them came yet and I don't understand. I'd ask why if I wasn't nonsensically moaning. They show me why. Rick sits on the chaise in front of me and pulls me forward until his cock is in my mouth. Boris is behind me and pulls my ass high into the air.

"Such a sweet ass, Serena. Never going to see it again without thinking of this view," he says.

Boris rams it into me, shoving Rick's cock into my throat. Being taken like this is very different. I feel like Boris is driving everything. He's got a death grip on my hips, yanking me back and forth while he drives down into me. He's forcing my husband into my throat with every thrust, making me take Rick deeper than ever. I thought my husband fucked me hard a moment ago, but Boris feels like he's trying to fuck through me. *Oh fuck, he's opening me up! He's so fucking thick!* The way he stretches my pussy is divine. I'm surprised Dina doesn't walk funny if she has this at home. I love my husband, but I think I could get addicted to getting fucked like this.

Rick isn't watching me choke on his dick. I'm looking up at him helplessly, but he looks over me, watching Boris screw me silly. The fire in his eyes is almost scary. Rick *loves* this. Has he always wanted to share me with another man? Why didn't he say anything? I don't think I'm the only one who could get addicted to Boris fucking me.

I'm not ready when Rick comes down my throat. Watching me being used is too much for my poor husband. I love that he's so turned on by watching me. I want his cum. I choke and he backs off, unloading more into my mouth. I'm too addled by Boris' thick cock to swallow. White cream seeps from where my lips are stretched around my husband. I'm a red-faced, drooling mess. Cum drips from my chin. Rick pulls out and smears cum across my lips and cheeks and nose. I must look a mess. *Did he want to see me like this?*

"Ahhh...ahhh...god...fuck...fuck meee..." I cry now that my mouth is free.

"Hot...tight...little pussy...goddam it...tight little fuck..." Boris grunts. I love hearing the strain in his voice. He's giving me everything he has, and I'm taking it.

"You love getting fucked," Rick growls, finally staring at me. My head rests on his thigh. His dick is in my face and part of me wants it back in my mouth so I can suck him back to life.

"Yess..."

"You need that big dick..."

"Yesss...I do...ahhh fuck..."

"Tell him, Serena! Tell him you need it!" Rick is animated like I've never seen.

"Fuck me! Fuck meee Booorisss! I need it! Ahhh...I...need it... fuck..."

"Uhnn...uhnn...you're a horny...little...slut...just like Dina said..."

"Yeah...fuck yeah...ahhh...I'm a horny...little slut...ahhh fuck...fuck me..." Just like Dina said? What the fuck? What did Dina say?

"You need that dick," Rick hisses. The guys are dirty talk tag teaming me.

"Ahhh yeah...I'm a horny slut...I need that dick...I need Boris' dick...Fuck...Fuck me...Ahhh fuck...I need your dick..."

"Hot...little...slut..."

Each word is punctuated with a deep, violent thrust. On *slut*, Boris is balls deep and unloads inside me. His sac is pressed against the backs of my thighs, and I feel him pulse while he pumps his powerful seed as deep inside me as he can get it. I should scream for him to pull out—Rick should demand he pulls out—but I tighten around him. My greedy pussy milks the thick, potent seed out of him like he's a bull here to breed me.

The cream filling me triggers my hardest orgasm of the night. It's so wrong that another man is coming inside me. Why do I love it so much? I'm howling, and Rick grabs his t-shirt from the patio and shoves it into my mouth. I howl harder. I truly love the rough treatment. It feels like Boris will never stop pumping cum into me.

Boris pulls out. I feel like I'll be stretched forever. My body quakes from the aftershocks of sweet pleasure rolling through me. *God, I never want to stop feeling like this!* Rick looks down at me with nothing but love in his eyes, and I don't understand how. He just watched me beg his best friend to fuck me. We've been together for nine years and he's never seen me be a slut like this. I smile, but his t-shirt is still stuffed in my mouth. I pull it out.

"Babe, I'm…" I pant.

"You're perfect, darling. I love you, Serena," Rick answers. He's perfect. He knows just what I need to hear.

Boris walks around with his slick dick swinging around. He fetches his phone and brings it over. Dina is on the screen in one of the bunks in the dark nurses' lounge. She looks as flushed as I feel.

"I didn't know you had that in you, Serena. That was hot," she says. Boris holds her close to my face. I'm still face down on the chaise.

"Did you just—uh—*enjoy yourself* at work?"

Dina smiles. "I just couldn't help myself. That was… fire. The three of you were incredible together."

"Thanks for sharing, I guess?"

"Anytime. I mean that too, as long as I get my quid pro quo."

I must still be high from coming so hard, so many times. Dina can't be saying what I think she's saying. "What do you mean?"

"Seriously Serena, you didn't think you'd just get to have your fun with the guys, and I'd be left out, did you? If you get them, I get them."

"That's fair," I admit, not liking it one bit anyway. I don't know that I can share Rick like she shared Boris. *Does my husband even want to fuck Dina?* That's a silly question. Everyone wants to fuck Dina. "We can talk about it."

Dina laughs. "We have a lot to talk about. We'll do lunch. Give me back to my husband."

Boris takes the phone away and walks off, leaving Rick and I alone. Suspicions come bubbling up. I feel like there was a plan, and I was the only one in the dark. I finally turn over and stretch my sore body. I feel like I've run a marathon.

"Was this planned?" I ask.

"Of course not," Rick replies. "How could I have planned this?"

"Maybe you and Boris talked. He talked to Dina."

"This was not planned. I couldn't have planned this. You know me better than that, Serena. It just happened."

"It just happened? You sharing me with Boris, while Dina sort of watched, just happened?"

"I swear. I did not plan this. I never thought in a million years something like this would or could happen."

"But you wanted it?"

Rick's wheels are turning. I know that look. "Wanted it? I don't know. It's a big thing. But have I thought about it? Yeah, I've fantasized about us having a threesome."

"Most guys want to be in the minority in that situation."

"That would be awesome too, if you and Dina ever want to…"

So, he does want to fuck her. Okay. "But you wanted *this* kind of threesome?"

Rick sighs. "Don't think I'm weird, okay? Yeah, something about the idea of seeing you getting fucked and losing control has always done it for me. You're the sexiest woman

I've ever met, Serena, and I guess I wanted to see you in action."

"Why didn't you ever say anything?"

"Because it's weird. You must think I'm weird now."

I climb up into his arms. "I don't think you're weird. Everyone has their fantasies. You're allowed to like what you like, babe." I think about how much I loved feeling Boris pump his load inside me. I still feel it in there, and slowly running onto my thighs. "I'll never judge you. I wish you'd told me."

"I think I would have if I'd known you were so eager to do it." He laughs.

"Are you judging me now?"

"Never, hon. I mean that in the best possible way."

"Maybe you are weird." I laugh. "But I love every weird bit of you, Rick. You're still my perfect man, and you always will be."

"Even after Boris railed you like that? I mean, you did say you *need* his dick."

"Stop it! That was heat of the moment dirty talk. You're the only man I need."

"But you'd fuck him again?"

I can't lie because I know he'll see right through me. "It was good, babe. If the circumstances were right, sure. A repeat wouldn't be the worst thing." Did I undersell it enough? "What about Dina? I think you just admitted you want to fuck her."

"I'm not sure I did, but sure, that would be a blast. How do you feel about that?"

"I don't know. Part of me is like, *hell no*. But I got this, and it wouldn't be fair to deny you. Dina expects it anyway, and she gets what she wants."

"She usually does," Rick agrees.

"I'll be jealous if it happens, but I'll be okay. I know you love me."

"I do."

"Just don't seem like you're too into it," I say, like I have any room to talk.

We both laugh.

Boris comes back over. He's off the phone and still naked. We're naked too, and I realize we should cover up. It's getting chilly now that I'm still anyway, but the hungry way he looks at me makes me want to stay naked. *God, am I becoming an attention whore?*

"Are you guys ready for round two?" he asks.

"That's up to the lady," Rick answers.

I don't know how I feel that my husband is ready to share me again so soon. I feel like we need more time to reconnect. I see the pulse in Boris' thick cock when he looks at me and reconsider. *How much would he fill me a second time?*

"Round two might kill me," I tell them. "I barely survived round one."

"Serena, you're a tigress. I think you could fuck both of us into an early grave."

"It would be fun to find out if that's true," Rick says. He does want this.

I look at each of the guys and knowing they both want me again triggers something inside me. I don't know how I'll handle the two of them again, but my body craves it. I guess I really am a horny slut. The guys might have broken something inside me.

"Why don't we go inside and freshen up, and see what happens?"

"Sounds like a plan," Rick agrees.

"Lead the way, Serena," Boris says.

Boris pulls me to my feet, and I take their hands and lead them into the house. Yeah, they're going to fuck me again. They're going to fuck me until they can't fuck anymore, and I'll beg for all of it. I'd owe Dina big for tonight, but she expects her own fun in return. I hope I can handle that.

Is this who we are now? Are we two couples who swap? *Are we swingers?* How many times does Rick want to watch me get fucked? How many men does he want to watch fuck me? I get chills thinking about it. We have so much to figure out, but for tonight, I'm going to let all of that go and just enjoy the two, thick cocks in front of me. I lead the boys straight up to the bedroom.

Kirsten McCurran is a pioneer in the hotwife erotica genre and the author of over 60 sexy books, including the recent bestsellers **Good Wives, Bad Behavior,** *and* **Sam Surrenders to the Neighbors.** *Book Two of her new series,* **Hannah Surrenders to the Landlords,** *will be released in May 2024. Find Kirsten's books at books. kirstenmccurran.com.*

ABOUT THE EDITOR

Kirsten McCurran is the pen name of a husband and wife team exploring the sexy secrets of middle-class, suburban couples. This couple has their own dirty little secret: they have lots of fantasies about what all their friends and neighbors are up to behind closed doors, and they turn those sexy fantasies into the stories they love to share with the world. The Mrs. could be the sweet mom you see in the stands at the soccer game or the pretty woman at the supermarket you wonder about as she's squeezing the melons. The Mr. could be your kid's little league coach.

Most of their stories are about married women looking to bust out and explore their wild side, often with the encouragement of their husbands—and sometimes without it. The strength of the couple behind Kirsten McCurran is that husband and wife writing together can uniquely capture the feelings of both partners in their couples as they explore their most forbidden desires. The Mrs. is all about exploring stories of daring women of a certain age exploring their sexuality, and the Mr. captures the feelings of the men who love them.

Kirsten McCurran has written over 60 ebooks, which can be found at major booksellers. You can reach Ms. McCurran on Twitter or by email at kmccurran@gmail.com. Find Kirsten's books at books.kirstenmccurran.com.

www.ingramcontent.com/pod-product-compliance
Lightning Source LLC
Chambersburg PA
CBHW071612150726
48000CB00004B/1698